TRUE TO YOUR SELFIE

MEGAN McCAFFERTY

SCHOLASTIC PRESS • NEW YORK

All rights reserved. Published by Scholastic Press, an imprint of Scholastic Inc., *Publishers since 1920*. SCHOLASTIC, SCHOLASTIC PRESS, and associated logos are trademarks and/or registered trademarks of Scholastic Inc.

The publisher does not have any control over and does not assume any responsibility for author or third-party websites or their content.

Library of Congress Cataloging-in-Publication Data available

ISBN 978-1-338-29699-0

10 9 8 7 6 5 4 3 2 1   20 21 22 23 24

Printed in the U.S.A.   23

First edition, February 2020

Book design by Yaffa Jaskoll

To Heather Schroder, for helping me
be the best version of myself

PART

ONE

MORGAN & ELLA

MY BEST FRIEND, MORGAN MIDDLETON, PUTS ON A smile she's worked very hard to master. It's the friendly Everygirl greeting: a silent, open-mouthed *"ohhhh hiiiiii"* inspired by Riley Quick, her pop star idol, who pioneered and perfected this look.

We're in our usual spot at the Mercer Community Pool Complex, facing the open swim area, a little too close to the greasy smog of the Snack Shack. It's not the most perfect spot—that would be the rows of umbrellas surrounding the high dives occupied by wild packs of high schoolers—but we're not even seventh graders yet. There's a lot of competition for lounge chairs, and at our age we're lucky to get them anywhere in the complex.

Since we arrived, we've been stalked by a quartet of nervous little girls who appear to be at least two years younger than we are, maybe more. I'm guessing eight to ten years old. Young enough that they wear one-piece swimsuits and still allow parents to apply thick layers of sunblock. Their faces are clear and makeup-free, their hair scraggly and damp with pool water. I can't decide if their lips are blue from Popsicles or playing Marco Polo too long.

I'm still not used to calling them our "fans."

The tallest girl is pushed to the front to represent the group.

"We love you!"

In public, we're a unit. So we reply in Morgan & Ella unison.

"And we love you!"

"Can we get a group selfie?"

"Of course you can!"

Our friend Maddy hops up from her chair and steps out of the shot. Earlier in the summer, she thought she'd be helpful by offering to take the picture for our fans. Morgan shut her down.

"Ummm . . . It's called a *selfie* not an *otherie*."

Then she made an exaggerated winky expression like a real-life emoji to make sure we all knew she was joking. That's another face Morgan has practiced a lot in the mirror. I appreciate her winky faces because otherwise I have a hard time knowing when Morgan is trying to be funny. She has a sophisticated sense of humor.

"You're both so pretty!" the tallest girl exclaims.

"Aw, thank you!" says Morgan & Ella.

"You know you're all beautiful too . . ." Morgan starts.

"In your own unique ways," I finish.

That's what Morgan & Ella always says when we're

complimented on our appearance. Morgan and I share a general category, twelve-almost-thirteen-year-old girls, but we don't look anything alike. Cake and pie share the same general category of dessert but are two very different things. Both yummy. But you wouldn't judge a pie by a cake's standards or vice versa. In sort of the same way it's impossible to decide who is prettier: Morgan or me. Or at least that's what Morgan says.

So far our fans seem to agree.

Morgan and I lean in to our fans like we're all best friends. The whole pack of them smells like pool chemicals and fake berry flavor.

"Hashtag Goalz Girlz!" cheers Morgan & Ella.

"Goalz Girlz!" our fans chant back.

clickclickclickclickclickclickclickclickclick

Duck pouts. Smizes. T. rex hands. We've got the poses down. Morgan deletes the uglies and enhances the pretties before returning the phone to the tallest one.

clickclickclickclickclickclickclickclickclick

"Follow Morgan & Ella on all the socials!" Maddy calls out to our fans as they skitter back to the other side of the pool.

Maddy is a terrible singer and was never in consideration for Morgan's on-screen partner. Fortunately for her, she's made herself useful by being a genius at market research and promotion.

"Hashtag Goalz Girlz! One word! With *z*'s!"

We are Morgan & Ella.

We record, edit, and post videos of ourselves singing covers of pop songs. Morgan sings lead. I play ukulele and sing harmony. Morgan & Ella has about ten thousand followers for each of the most important socials, like Insta, Snap, and Fotobomb. Every time I get a little freaked out by so many eyeballs, Morgan reminds me that we're tiny compared to the most popular influencers. That's true, but ten thousand is waaaaay more than the number of students, teachers, and parents in the audience at Shadybrook Elementary School's talent show. Outside of Mercer, New Jersey, we aren't celebrities yet. But we are to the little girls at the pool. And they are just the beginning.

"They're our *first* fans." Morgan waves at them. "But not the last!"

Morgan blows on her sunglasses and hands them to Maddy.

"Those little girls will have big-time bragging rights when our videos go viral," Morgan continues. "All we need is a shout-out from the right influencer . . ."

"Click, click, click, BOOM! All over the internet!" exclaims Maddy.

Maddy cleans the lenses with a special cloth, then hands the sunglasses back to Morgan. The frames are flamingo pink, which I thought would clash with her red hair, but nope, the colors totally pop on camera. Morgan always selfie-tests before buying anything. Luckily for me, she gets bored with her purchases and happily passes them on. At least half the clothes on my floor once hung in Morgan's walk-in closet.

"Our fans need a name for themselves," Morgan says.

"What do you mean?" I ask.

"Riley Quick has Ribots," Maddy explains. "Kaytee K. has Kayters. The Morgan & Ella fandom needs a name."

"It really should be priority number one." Morgan swipes on her phone.

I automatically reach for my phone in my bag so I can start swiping too.

"What about Ukies?" Maddy suggests. "For the ukulele?"

Morgan frowns, gives a thumbs-down.

"Rhymes with pukies. And puts too much focus on Ella."

"Reddies?" Maddy suggests. "For your hair?"

Morgan smiles and tosses her flame-colored curls over her shoulder but reluctantly gives another thumbs-down.

"But I like where you're going with this."

As Morgan and Maddy pitch potential nicknames for our tiny-but-growing fan base, I close my eyes and put my own priorities in order.

1. Avoid The Eyeroll.
2. Be good for Mom.
3. Listen to my sister, Lauren.

I'm working on number four when Morgan spritzes me with cucumber water hydrating mist. I can't see through the mirrored lenses of her sunglasses, but I'm pretty sure I've already failed at number one.

"You've been very quiet during our brainstorming session."

I've been very quiet because it's impossible to deliver on the first priority and still come through on the second and third. I don't know why Morgan wants my opinion anyway. She is smart. Like, *the way the world works* smart. She is also school smart.

I am neither.

Okay, that's not totally accurate. I am pretty good at all the parts of school that don't have anything to do with learning, studying, or test taking. The less it has to do with any of those things, the better I am at it. I'm not playing dumb like some people I know. *Boo-hoo! I got an A minus in Advanced Quantum Calculus of Geometric Astrophysics!* No. I've got years of not-great report cards to back me up. Some Satisfactories, some Unsatisfactories. Many Needs Improvements. The only Outstandings I ever got were in music classes.

And it's not like I'm *diagnosably* not-great at school either. My mom is in the medical field, so you can bet I've been tested, but I don't have ADHD or dyslexia. I don't have any learning disabilities, although Lauren says not putting anything away means I've got an episode of *Hoarders* in my future. I'm just, like, *normal* not-great at school, which makes my not-great-at-schooling very frustrating for Mom. This year I would like to be better than not-great at school (see priorities number two and number three). But pleasing Morgan (priority number one) takes up a lot of time and energy, and there are only so many hours in the day.

"Maybe we should focus a little less on stardom," I suggest, "and a little more on starting seventh grade."

Morgan lowers her sunglasses. "Seventh grade? Really?"

I clutch the arms of my chair to brace myself for The Eyeroll as epic as the earth's orbit around the sun. The Eyeroll that can be seen from outer space. The Eyeroll with cosmic consequences.

"Why do you think so small, Ella?"

I think so small because The Eyeroll means I am an insignificant speck in Morgan Middleton's universe.

Morgan sighs deeply, but The Eyeroll doesn't come.

"I'm already in with all the most popular eighth-grade girls because of travel soccer. And you're the younger sister of a Mercer High School soccer star. We'd have nothing to worry about even if our Fotobomb wasn't blowing up, which it *totally* is."

"What about me?" Maddy asks. "What do I have going for me?"

"Duh! You're friends with us!"

Then Morgan ding-dongs her head in the back-and-forth way she does whenever Maddy or I say anything *too* ditzy for the brand. This gesture is playful so it doesn't have anywhere near the same devastating effect as The Eyeroll. What a relief to finally have a best friend who doesn't push me to be any smarter than I need to be but also discourages me from acting less smart than I really am. I don't like questioning Morgan's expertise, but I still can't help but ask.

"How can you be so sure?"

Fortunately, Morgan enjoys this opportunity to assert her authority. She sits up tall in her chair, a regal pose for Mercer, New Jersey, royalty.

"Because I am a Middleton," she says. "And Middletons are winners."

Morgan's mother was made the first female partner at her law firm because Middletons are *winners*. Morgan's father moved up from town councilman to mayor to congressman because Middletons are *winners*. Morgan has been watching her parents win cases and elections her whole life.

"I'm not a Middleton," I say, pointing out the obvious.

"But you're a Middleton's best friend!" Maddy replies eagerly. "Which is the next best thing to being one!"

"Listen to Maddy," Morgan says. "She's the *next best* next best thing."

And when Morgan winks we all know it's okay to laugh at the joke.

Most almost-thirteen-year-olds would happily settle for being the most popular girls in seventh grade. Until my first time on the receiving end of The Eyeroll, I would've happily settled for not being the most *un*popular girl in seventh grade. But Morgan Middleton isn't most almost-thirteen-year-olds. And now that I've been chosen as her BFF, neither am I. For Morgan & Ella, Mercer Middle School popularity is just a formality to pass through on the way to what Morgan calls "global multiplatform domination." Morgan calls herself the Girlboss Goddess Next Door, which is pretty funny because nobody lives next door to her. Her family's estate is the only house on the block, an ivy-covered mansion hidden behind a security wall. This could be off-putting to our fans if Morgan weren't so humble.

"It's so important to be humble," she likes to remind me. "Name another girl who has *so* much and stays *so* humble."

I can't. Morgan is the humblest.

At all times, I'm expected to embody the Goofball Goddess role Morgan has assigned to me. I love singing, playing the ukulele, and making videos, but maintaining this image can be very stressful. That's why Morgan takes all the guesswork out of status-making or -breaking decisions about wardrobe, hair, and makeup.

"It's time for you to up your nail game, Ella," Morgan announces.

Playing the ukulele puts a lot of wear and tear on my nails. Any cute polish I put on gets scratched off within minutes of strumming. Chipped polish not only looks bad on camera but can actually have an effect on the sound made by the strings. So far I've opted out, hoping Morgan would understand why without my having to explain: Perfect nails cost too much money to maintain.

"My assistant is taking us for mani-pedis the day after tomorrow."

Izzy used to be Morgan's nanny. About six months ago Morgan started referring to her as "my assistant."

"But . . ." I start to protest.

"My treat!" Morgan insists. "We're a team! What's good for you is good for me is good for Morgan & Ella!"

And before I can say anything more, Morgan has already moved on to a monologue about a boy she's had her eye on since he showed up at the pool a few weeks ago. "The Mystery Hottie" is not here today. His absence, Morgan says, is *tragic*, and Maddy wholeheartedly agrees. I barely remember who they're talking about, but I go along with the gossip because it's more fun than being left out of the conversation.

Not for the first time this summer, I find myself asking the following question: If I weren't half of Morgan & Ella, what would I be doing right now?

You'd be splashing around the pool with those little girls you call "fans."

Oh no. It's The Best Friend in My Head.

You'd stay in the water until your lips turned blue and your fingers went pruny. And when you finally got out, you'd spread your towel under the leafy maple tree and swap old copies of the Dragonologist Chronicles . . .

That's what I did last summer. And the summer before that and before that. Baby stuff was fine back in elementary school. But we're older now, about to start middle school and . . .

Those summers are gone.

Yes. Those summers are gone. Morgan chose me and I chose her in return.

Over Sophie.

Over me, says The Best Friend in My Head.

This time I don't argue back.

Yes, I silently reply. *Over you.*

DISASTER

LESS THAN TWENTY-FOUR HOURS LATER, MORGAN is stomping across my bedroom, trampling right over the laundry—dirty, clean, doesn't matter now—in her platform flip-flops.

"This is a disaster, Ella!"

Like everything she's passionate about, Morgan is totally committed to pacing and can't be bothered to kick away clothes to clear a path. It's totally my fault for scattering stuff all over the floor in the first place. But since my sister left for college a few weeks ago, I'm taking full advantage of having a bedroom to myself. For the first time in my life, I can be as messy as I want to be.

"I cannot believe you lost your phone!"

After all the work we've put in this summer. All the practicing and planning, studying and strategizing. How could I be so careless so close to the start of seventh grade at Mercer Middle School? How could I jeopardize the future of Morgan & Ella's global multiplatform domination?

"When you didn't reply to my Morning Must-Dos, I thought, okay, Ella can't text back because she couldn't wait another day to fix those janky nails!"

Morgan wiggles silver glitter fingertips at me. I sit on my hands, too guilty to even look at my naked nails.

Morgan spins, begins another lap.

"But when I factored in drying time and you still hadn't responded to my texts, I started to get worried. Like, seriously worried."

If we were at her house, Morgan would have enough square mileage to really work up an anxious sweat. But the bedroom I shared with my sister is smaller than Morgan's walk-in closet. She barely goes three paces before she has to double back over my dirty laundry.

"I started to think that maybe you had *died*, Ella." Morgan goes still, presses a hand to her heart. "Like, seriously dead, died."

I have this superannoying nervous habit of bursting into inappropriate giggles at Morgan's most serious moments. I press my lips together to stop it from happening again.

"I had your memorial ready to launch across all the socials," Morgan continues. "Ella Jane Plaza: My BFF As Only I Knew Her."

Sneaky laughter snurgles through my nose.

SNNNNNNOOOOOORRRRRRT.

Morgan has warned me that snorting like a hog will make all the boys think I'm more piggy than pretty. This, she has said, would be a tragic waste of cuteness. Fortunately, she's too caught up in my near-death experience to get upset about that right now.

"It was beautiful. All of Morgan & Ella's most loved and linked moments." Morgan sighs. "Our winning medley of Riley Quick songs at the Jersey Fresh Talent Showcase. Our stirring rendition of 'The Star-Spangled Banner' at the BlueClaws baseball game. Our first video to break ten thousand views!"

She stops reminiscing about my online funeral and picks up a crumpled Dragonologist Chronicles T-shirt at her feet. She pinches it like it's a sack of actual dragon poop.

"Ummm?"

"I wear it to sleep!"

"What happened to the cute PJs I gave you?" she asks. "With the ice-cream cones and kittens?"

I'm lactose intolerant and allergic to cats. Those pajamas are a tribute to farts and sneezes, but she doesn't care. Cuteness > Everything Else.

"They're around here somewhere."

I optimistically turn over the nearest pillow, hoping by some miracle to find the pajamas and my phone. I am— unsurprisingly—disappointed.

"Never, ever, *ever* show up to school wearing that shirt."

"I promise!"

I will never wear it again. Not even to sleep. That shirt is deader to me than (SPOILER ALERT!!!) FlutterFyre in book six.

"I'm worried that you're slipping back into bad fashion habits," Morgan says. "Make it part of your routine to ask yourself: *Does this outfit honor the Goofball Goddess within?*"

I have no clue what honors the Goofball Goddess within. Only Morgan knows, which makes sense because she's the Girlboss Goddess. This is why I need the Morning Must-Dos to guide me through my days.

Morgan answers her own question by flinging the offending shirt into the corner. It hits the bookshelf holding the entire Dragonologist Chronicles series including all the companion maps and guidebooks. I haven't browsed those books or any others in . . . well . . . a while.

It drove Lauren nuts that my half of the bookshelf was taken over by a library of barely-used cosmetics and off-trend accessories. In less than a year, I've put together an impressive beautification collection: gloppy pots of lip gloss and half-cracked cakes of bronzer, broken choker necklaces, beadless bracelets, and earrings missing their matches. My sister's hair is *always* in a ponytail. Her idea of a bold lip is cherry-flavored ChapStick. So it's no surprise she thinks mastering winged eyeliner is a waste of my time. Cramming for exams and kicking a soccer ball are important to Lauren's future. Morgan insists that experimenting with different looks is just as important to mine.

I mean *ours*.

"Why didn't you just tell me you lost your phone?" Morgan asks.

I couldn't tell you I lost my phone, I think, *because I didn't want to let you down.*

"I couldn't tell you I lost my phone," I answer, "because I lost my phone."

"Ummm . . ." Morgan tilts her head askew. "There are these things? Called laptops? That are just like phones? Only bigger?"

"My sister took the laptop to college. And the desktop computer is for Mom's work only. I don't even know the password."

"Riiiiight."

"I'm like a seventh grader in the nineties," I say.

Mom loves reminding me that when she was my age her only form of communication was a landline phone connected to the wall. The twisty cord could be pulled from the kitchen down the hall but always fell short just outside Mom's bedroom door. No matter how hard she tried, she couldn't stretch it another foot or two to give herself some privacy. And if Grandma was already on the line, she'd have to wait patiently until she finished her conversation. And it could be literally *hours* before Grandma hung up, because back then everyone timesucked by talking on the phone-in-the-wall in the same way we timesuck by posting selfies, memes, and comments on Fotobomb. And when Grandma finally, finally got off the phone, Mom could call her best friend and get a busy signal, which was the worst because she had no way of knowing when the line would be free, so she'd have to redial *all the digits*, like, every thirty seconds until she finally got through. And by that time, Mom had a broken finger from all the button pushing and probably forgot what she wanted to tell her friend anyway.

When Mom makes time to tell stories about her youth, there's a guaranteed lesson to be learned. This one went something like this:

"At your age, everything feels urgent, but it's probably not."

There's no way I can share Mom's wisdom with Morgan at this moment.

"Losing your phone sets us back thirty years!" Morgan punts a pillow across the room. "Thanks for summing up why this is such a *disaster*!"

"You're welcome?"

Morgan does not reward me with a laugh.

HATERS

MORGAN IS DETERMINED TO MAKE CONTACT WITH the Mystery Hottie before summer is over, so we're back at the Mercer Community Pool Complex. As instructed to do in our absence, Maddy has put down towels *and* stretched her body horizontally across our lounge chairs to prevent anyone from taking over the territory we've carefully claimed as our own this summer.

"Yoo-hoo! Morgan! Ella!"

Maddy jumps up when she sees us but doesn't abandon the chairs. Not even for a second. Just a few days are left before the pool closes for the season, but Morgan says we can't let our guards down now. You never know when haters might try to take what's ours.

"Where were you? Are you okay? Why didn't you text back?"

Maddy has texted Morgan no fewer than fifty times in the last half hour. She's vibrating with worry.

"It's a disaster, Maddy. A *disaster*!"

Morgan faints into her chair. With her pale skin and red hair, she's always less than thirty seconds away from a total-body sun blister, so I can't blame her for snagging the chaise under full protection of the umbrella. "From this spot, I can take and throw shade at the same time," Morgan said on the first pool day of the summer.

"What happened?" Maddy asks breathlessly.

Maddy fans Morgan with the September issue of *Vogue* that inspired us to dream out loud about the perfect photo shoot. I saw us performing in front of a screaming audience of thousands, styled in bedazzled bodysuits that glittered like diamonds in the stage lights. Morgan went bigger, of course. Much bigger. She saw us as alien warrior princesses "attacking intergalactic tackiness," as she put it, dressed in luxury designers with foreign names I'd never heard of and couldn't pronounce even if I had. Morgan's vision is not limited to this earth.

"Do you want to tell Maddy, or should I?"

It's a non-question. We all know Morgan is much better at sharing drama than I am. So I roll my towel into a pillow, recline, and let her tell Maddy everything she needs to know about The Disaster of the Day: Ella's Lost Phone. I'm trying not to stress too much about the loss, or having to tell Mom when she gets home from work, or Lauren after Mom texts her at college to complain about my carelessness.

I tilt my face toward the sun . . .

Ella!

. . . and that's when I hear the familiar voice for the first time today.

The Best Friend in My Head. Or the ex–best friend, I should say, since we haven't hung out in many, many months.

You really should apply sunscreen. Put on a hat. Avoid direct exposure between ten a.m. and four p.m.

"So how will Ella get the Morning Must-Dos?" Maddy asks Morgan.

Tanning without burning is still sun damage, The Best Friend in My Head continues in that know-it-all tone of hers. *You may have inherited olive skin from your Mediterranean ancestors, but you can still get melanoma, the deadliest of all skin cancers.*

"How will she update the socials?" Maddy asks.

I feel better with a tan! I silently argue back. *I look better with a tan!*

When The Best Friend in My Head fights back with threats of saggy skin and wrinkles, I scooch my chair under the umbrella.

Happy now?

I'm just looking out for you, says The Best Friend in My Head.

I don't need you looking out for me anymore, I think. *I've got Morgan.*

"How will she maintain the Morgan & Ella *brand*?"

No one goes from zero to zero chill faster than Maddy. Her

tryharding gets on Morgan's nerves, which is why I work super-hard at being totally chill all the time.

"Are you *sure* you lost your phone?" Maddy asks me.

"I'm sure!" I reply. "We searched the whole *disaster* zone up and down."

"Fortunately, Ella's room is tiny," Morgan says. "Omigoddess! Imagine how long it would take to search *my* room?"

"Maybe it wasn't lost," Maddy thinks out loud. "Maybe it was *stolen*!"

I expect Morgan to laugh right in her face because that's what she does when Maddy gets too hyper. But she surprises me by going all in on the conspiracy theory.

"Omigoddess! What if she's right?" Morgan asks. "What if someone stole your phone? What if a hater is hacking into Morgan & Ella's socials right now?"

Morgan and Maddy whip out their phones and start scroll-ing. I reach for mine, too, before remembering I don't know where it is. Mom will not be happy to hear I've lost such an expensive gift, especially after I pleaded and promised I could be trusted with it, like Morgan and Maddy and all the other girls my age who've already had phones for, like, ever. Lauren will take a break from being an awesome student athlete to lecture me about how sloppy and irresponsible I am, and I'll miss her even more than I already do. This doesn't make any sense, but that's what happens when you get used to falling asleep to the sound of your sister's breathing.

"Everything looks okay," Maddy says reassuringly.

"What if the hacker is waiting until peak posting hours for maximum damage?" Morgan turns to me. "You deleted the uglies, right? Please tell me you deleted the uglies as I've been telling you to do for months now . . ."

For every approved pretty (bright eyes, highlighted cheekbones, just-right nose, shiny hair, glossy lips) there are at least a dozen uglies (puffy eyes, double chins, weird nostrils, limp hair, dingy teeth).

"*You* deleted all the uglies," I remind her. "You didn't trust me to do it myself."

"We are *so* done if those uglies go viral," Morgan says. "Gigi from Fourth Dimension was forced to go on a social media blackout for *eighteen whole days* after her phone was hacked and the whole world saw those hot mess snaps at the Grammys after-party and . . ."

"But then she cleaned herself up and came back as the brand ambassador for Frootie Smoothie," I point out. "And now Gigi has more Fotobomb followers than all the other girls in the group combined."

When Morgan skeptically purses her lips, Maddy quickly shows her the Fotobomb numbers, proving me right.

"There's no such thing as bad publicity," Maddy says.

For the next few seconds, Morgan silently scrolls through the socials while Maddy and I watch. We know not to interrupt her when she's thinking.

"Hmmm," Morgan says finally. "We'll see if you're right about that."

A PLACE FOR EVERYTHING

I'VE LOST TRACK OF THE HOURS. IT'S JUST IZZY and me in the SUV, because she's already delivered Morgan to wherever she needs to be. This happens a lot, because Morgan has many places to go and I do not.

We post on all the socials once a week, which Morgan says is not nearly enough new content to grow our fan base. According to Maddy's research, we should be recording, editing, and posting new songs *at least* twice a week in addition to more frequent quickie "lifestyle" updates. Morgan is way busier than I am with travel soccer, hip-hop dance class, and horseback riding, but I went a little too far when I hinted that her schedule might be more disruptive to Morgan & Ella's video making than mine.

"If it weren't for *my* camera, *my* mics, *my* lights, *my* editing software, *my vision*," she reminded me, "there wouldn't be *any* Morgan & Ella videos!"

It's hard to argue with Morgan when she's right. It's even harder to argue with Morgan when she's wrong, because she's never wrong. She reminds me of my sister, Lauren, in that way. I envy both of them for being so certain about everything all the time.

Anyway, being left alone with Izzy is usually okay, because she drives and I mess around on my phone and we smile politely at each other but aren't expected to make conversation. But today it feels more awkward than usual because I don't have my phone or anything else to distract myself during the ride. I stare at the back of Izzy's head and count nine wiry gray hairs starting at her scalp and winding around the black bun at the nape of her neck. She's not old but not young either. She's probably in her late thirties, around the same age as Mom. I hope Izzy gets paid extra for not only being Morgan's chauffeur but mine too.

When Izzy pulls up to the apartment, Mom's car is parked in the reserved spot out front. It must be after seven p.m. but before eight p.m.—what Lauren calls the "magic hour" between Mom's work and night class.

"Thank you, Izzy," I say.

"You're welcome, Ella," she replies. "Pick you up at ten tomorrow! No pool. Spa day!"

I appreciate the reminder. Izzy knows Morgan & Ella's schedule better than I do.

I sniff deeply as I approach the apartment, trying to detect garlic, basil, or other spices in the air. I really hope Mom hasn't gone out of her way to make a nice dinner for me, because Morgan insisted we stop for iced coffees and cupcakes. Our fans love photos of us posing with iced coffees and cupcakes.

The front door flies open.

"Ella Jane Plaza! Where have you been?"

Mom is still in her scrubs, the deep purple ones that go with her Violet Twist lip gloss. An appreciation of makeup is one of the few things the two of us have in common that Lauren does not. Mom can't be too fashionable as an occupational therapist assistant, but she likes to match her lip look to her work clothes. She usually changes as soon as she gets home, but I guess she was too worried about me.

"I was with Morgan . . ."

"I know that!" She gives Izzy a quick little wave as the Mercedes pulls away. "But I didn't know *where* you were with Morgan! Why didn't you reply to my texts?"

There goes any hope of putting off the truth.

"I . . ."

Mom's purple lips get even twistier than usual.

"I . . ."

Mom slaps a palm to her forehead.

"It's lost," she says. "You lost your phone."

And I barely muster a guilty little nod before she turns on her rubber clogs and marches right back into the apartment. No signs or smells of dinner, so at least I don't have to feel even worse about Mom making a meal I'm too full to eat.

"I should have listened to your sister," Mom says wearily on the way to her bedroom. "She said you weren't responsible enough for your own phone. She said you were too disorganized. And she was right."

Lauren is always right.

I choke down the teary burn building up in the back of my throat. I don't want Mom to see me cry. Not when she has to leave for class very soon to get there on time.

"It still might turn up," I say. "I haven't looked everywhere . . ."

Mom releases the topknot and shakes out her curls. My hair is the same shade, but Mom's TresSupreme Brown Sugar Premium Color comes from a box. Whenever she dyes her hair, she laughs about how having Lauren at eighteen made her go prematurely gray. My mom has always been the youngest— and, in my eyes, prettiest—mom on the playground, in the audience, at back-to-school nights.

She shimmies out of her scrubs and pulls on a pair of jeans. Then she asks the question she always asks when I lose something, which is often.

"Where's the last place you put it?"

If I knew the answer to that question—this and every time she asks—the lost thing wouldn't be lost. But I don't say that. Instead I make a suggestion based on what she'll say next.

"I'll retrace my steps."

Mom pops her head out of a sleeveless V-neck sweater.

"That's a great idea."

She grabs a ginormous textbook titled *A Field Guide to Physical Dysfunction* and slides it into her backpack. "If I can carry this book around," Mom likes to joke when she's got time for jokes, "I'll have no trouble lifting my elderly clients." But she doesn't have time for jokes tonight.

"You okay with frozen pizza? There's leftover salad in the fridge."

"I'm fine."

Mom scoops up her car keys from the wobbly blue dish on the hall table closest to the front door. A ceramics project from Lauren's second grade art class, it's been used exclusively for holding keys ever since. Mom and Lauren never lose keys, phones, or anything else. They live by the motto "a place for everything and everything in its place." They cannot understand why I can't follow their orderly example. I don't understand either.

"I'm sorry about my phone," I say.

Mom stops. She sighs. She presses her lips to the top of my head.

"I know you are, sweetie," she says. "I know you are."

She reminds me about the frozen pizza and the leftover salad. She reminds me to lock the door behind her and not to open it up for anyone. She reminds me of the neighbors I can go to in case of an emergency. She reminds me that she will be home by eleven p.m. She reminds me that she's got two semesters left before she gets her degree and a higher-paying job. She reminds me that she loves me.

And then I watch her go.

"Alone again," I say to the empty apartment.

I gently tap my fingers across my scalp and, as always, I'm comforted by the glossy kiss Mom left behind.

COMPROMISE

FOR THE FIRST TIME IN MONTHS, I WAKE UP NATU-rally, without the chirpy ping of Morgan's Must-Dos. I automatically reach for my cell anyway, as I've done at least a millionbilliontrillion times in the last day. Without clear instructions from Morgan, I'm feeling as lost as my phone. Before we became best friends, I checked my daily horoscope in the newspaper for guidance. Maybe Sydney Stargazer can let me and all the other Aquarians know what we're in for today.

Mom has already cleared her breakfast plate and is finishing up her coffee when I shuffle into the kitchen. I don't see a newspaper anywhere in sight. Now that I think of it, I'm pretty sure Mom canceled our daily subscription to the *Mercer Observer* to save money. Well, so much for help from Sydney Stargazer.

"Good morning, sleepyhead!" Mom says. "I thought I'd have to yank you out from under the covers!"

Mom never leaves for work without waking me up first. I'm usually an early riser, but I haven't been sleeping so well since Lauren left. I pretended to be out cold when Mom checked in on me after she got home from class last night. It seemed easier than telling her I hadn't found my phone.

I stayed up late practicing all the new covers Morgan wants to record next, half of which aren't obvious ukulele songs and don't even have tabs for me to learn from. But I don't mind, because it's actually more fun when I have to figure out for myself how to turn dubstep bleep-blorping into plucking. I didn't even mute the strings, because Mom grew up in Brooklyn and can sleep through car alarms, trash compactors, and police sirens. But if I ever tried to sneak out in the middle of the night, you can bet she'd already be at the front door blocking my exit. She's got selective hearing in that hyper-protective Mom kind of way.

"Any luck finding your phone?" she asks.

I can't pretend to be asleep, so I shrug instead. Mom doesn't conceal her disappointment.

"I hate to bother Izzy," she says, "but I'll have to text her if I can't reach you."

I pick up the first box of cereal, pour it into my bowl.

"I don't think Izzy will mind," I say. "She likes me."

I pick up a second box of cereal, pour it into my bowl.

"I'm sure she likes you. But it's not her job to be in charge of you too . . ."

Mom's voice trails off. Izzy has pretty much been in charge of me all summer. Hanging out with Morgan was far cheaper than any summer camp I didn't want to go to anyway. With only a few days left until school starts, it's a little too late for Mom to regret this arrangement.

"So," Mom says, stirring a spoon around her mug, "what are you and Morgan up to today? The pool?"

"No," I reply. "Izzy is taking us for mani-pedis."

Mom stops stirring, frowns.

"I'm not asking you for money! Morgan likes treating me . . ."

"I know," Mom says. "Morgan is very generous, but . . ."

"But what?" I ask.

"It makes me uncomfortable," she says simply.

I understand what she means. I still get freaked out when I think about how wealthy Morgan's family is. I'm pretty sure our entire two-bedroom apartment could fit inside the Middletons' six-car garage. I almost died of embarrassment the first time Morgan showed up here unannounced. She totally picked up on my mortification and immediately put me at ease.

"If my parents didn't want me to be friends with girls like you who live in apartments like this, they'd put me in Ivy Academy or some other snobby private school," she said. "Now show me that ukulele!"

32

My chosen instrument had Morgan's full approval. She called it "quirky cute."

"It totally fits your Goofball Goddess aesthetic," Morgan decided.

"I have an . . . *aesthetic*?"

I made sure to pronounce it the same way she did. It was one of those words I'd seen on the socials but never heard out loud. I had never considered developing an aesthetic until Morgan made it seem as necessary as oxygen for survival.

"Of course you have an aesthetic! We both do!" Morgan laughed. "You're the Goofball Goddess, and I'm the Girlboss Goddess. We can't get famous without an aesthetic!"

"We're going to be famous?"

"Of course we're going to be famous!" Morgan wasn't laughing anymore. "Think of this as the *pre-famous* phase of our lives."

Most moms would be thrilled if their daughter was in with Mercer Middle School's biggest influencer. But my mom is not most moms. She thinks Morgan is too superficial and too obsessed with the socials. Worst of all, she thinks Morgan has an unrealistic view of the world and my role in it.

I defend our friendship for the millionbilliontrillionth time.

"If I had money, I'd treat her," I reply. "That's what friends do."

"But you don't," Mom says, looking into her mug. "And you can't."

I have nothing positive to say about this, so I shovel in a

huge mouthful of "Compromise" instead of talking. That's what Lauren calls the fifty-fifty bland nutritious/sugary delicious cereal combo I eat for breakfast every day. Today it's whole grain Shredded Wheat and Apple Jacks.

Mom throws back the rest of the coffee and stands. She's rinsing out her mug in the sink when she snaps her fingers like she's suddenly just remembered something.

"Guess who I saw yesterday on my drive home from the hospital!" She doesn't wait for me to guess. "Sophie!"

I poke a spoon around the bowl of Compromise. The soy milk is turning a peachy color not all that different from Mom's scrubs or matching Sherbet Surprise lip gloss. Soy milk costs twice as much as regular milk, so I try to pour just enough to cover Compromise and no more.

"She was coming out of the hardware store dragging a trash can filled with gardening supplies."

The hardware store? Of course that's where Sophie goes for all her back-to-school shopping.

"How did she spend her summer?" Mom asks.

I shrug again.

"You haven't seen her at the pool?"

"Nope."

That's mostly true. Sophie made one appearance early in the season.

She and I used to race each other to be the first to jump in the deep end. So when I dared her to cannonball, she didn't hesitate. Even after everything that had happened between us in sixth grade, she still believed me when I said I'd take the plunge too. But I stopped short of the edge and watched her hit the water all by herself. She came up for air to the sound of Morgan's laughter. She says public pools are like "human soup." Gross. Anyone who swims in them is gross by association. Unless you're a cute boy like the Mystery Hottie. Then it's okay. Cute boys like the Mystery Hottie can break all the rules.

"I come here for the social scene," Morgan reminded us whenever Maddy complained about the heat. "If I wanted to swim, I'd just stay home."

So that explained why Morgan loved hanging out *at* the pool but never *in* it.

And also why Sophie didn't show up again for the rest of the summer.

"Sophie's a good girl," Mom says. "She's got her head on straight."

"Yeah, I know," I say.

"She's a good friend for you," Mom says. "Lauren thinks so too."

And Lauren's always right.

"Maybe you and Morgan can record one of your videos with her?"

I laugh out loud, spraying soy milk and half-chewed cereal all over my place mat.

"That's not happening, Mom."

"Why not?" Mom hands me a paper towel to clean up the

mess I was ready to sop up with my sleeve. "You two always blended so well."

Before Morgan & Ella there was Ella and Sophie. Two girls who were best friends. We also sang together, but it wasn't for fame and fortune and followers. We weren't motivated by international stardom. We sang together because between kindergarten and sixth grade we did *everything* together.

"I miss seeing Sophie around here," Mom says.

We haven't hung out in almost a year, and yet I still hear Sophie's voice more clearly than my own.

Don't you miss me too? she asks.

I'm not even hungry, but I choke down more Compromise. Anything to stop myself from shouting *SHUT UP! SHUT UP! SHUT UP!* at Mom, Lauren, and The Best Friend in My Head.

OMIGODDESS

I SHOULD'VE KNOWN THAT A RANDOM STRIP MALL mani-pedi place was not Morgan Middleton's style. Namaste Day Spa, as Morgan mentioned, then reminded me at least three times on the half-hour drive, was featured in *Vogue* as "New Jersey's number one Members-only destination for mind-body rejuvenation."

It's already working on Morgan. She's high-key loving every second of this majorly postable afternoon. She's already shared pics of Morgan & Ella:

1. Striking "om" poses
2. Strutting runway style in our bathrobes
3. Admiring each other's towel turbans
4. Making monster faces while wearing green tea detoxifying masks

clickclickclickclickclickclickclickclickclick

The little girls at the pool—our fans—are totally into it. Morgan & Ella's socials are all lit up with loves that I can't see because I still don't have my phone. Morgan isn't even annoyed about doing all the work because she's way better at the socials than I am anyway.

"This is the best practice for spon con." Morgan slips her phone into the front pocket of her robe. "It won't be long until they're paying us to get treatments!"

She leans back in her lounge chair, sighs, and closes her eyes. Business done, Morgan is totally blissing out.

I'm totally stressing out.

For one thing, our private sanctuary is decorated like, I don't know? A rain forest? And there are definitely too many tropical plants near too many lit candles.

This place is a fire trap, warns The Best Friend in My Head.

And as much as I want to disagree with her, I make note of the exits.

"I'm Patty. Your personal aesthetician for the afternoon."

Patty's bun is pulled so tight it tugs her skin taut across her cheekbones. I can't tell if she's twenty or forty.

"Aesthetician." I pronounce it carefully to get it right. "As in aesthetics."

Patty smiles blankly.

"I'm Ella," I say.

"It's nice to meet you, Ella," Patty says. "We always welcome guests of Miss Middleton."

"She's never been to a spa before," Morgan says as one of her PAs puts cucumber slices on her eyes.

Morgan doesn't know the full truth: I've never had a real manicure, not even from a cheapo nail salon, let alone a luxury Members-only day spa featured in *Vogue*.

"Let's see what I'm working with here."

Patty glances at my hands and frowns.

"So uneven."

She's just stating the truth. The nails on my right hand are noticeably longer than on my left.

"Unnnnh."

Her disapproval sounds like a loogie lodged in the back of her throat. She'd be much happier with Morgan, who has a total of three personal aestheticians literally waiting on her hand and foot. None of these young women bear any resemblance to Mom, but I'm reminded of her anyway. Their matching Namaste uniforms—loose-fitting, bright orange-and-pink batik-print cotton tops and drawstring pants—aren't all that different from the scrubs she wears to work.

"Unnnnnnnnh."

Now Patty is grimacing at the thick calluses on my left hand, the one I use to press the strings down on the frets.

Patty's fretting, jokes The Best Friend in My Head, *over fretting.*

The Best Friend in My Head never cares if I am in the right mood to appreciate puns. But she's right. Morgan's PAs all smile peacefully as they massage something called coconut basil balm butter onto her hands and feet. But Patty shoves my hands into the soapy water like they're a crusty burnt casserole dish that needs scrubbing.

"Soak to soften!"

I pull them out.

Patty pushes them back in.

I pull them back out.

"Miss Middleton! Why is your *guest* fighting me?"

I can't help but notice Patty's emphasis on the word "guest." Morgan is a capital *M* Member. I am a lowercase guest.

Morgan groans, sits up, and removes the slices of cucumber from her eyes.

"What now?"

"It's just . . ." I begin.

"It's just *what*, Ella?" Morgan says. "This spa was featured in *Vogue*. What could be wrong?"

"It's . . ."

"Do you know how badly Maddy wanted to be my plus-one?" Morgan asks. "Like, really bad."

I don't want to seem ungrateful. I realize that bringing me here is a big deal. But when I agreed to a manicure, I didn't expect all this. I thought I'd get a tiny trim, a little shaping, and a few coats of the strongest polish that met Morgan's standards for on-cam cuteness. I didn't know the manicurist—I mean, my personal aesthetician—would set out to destroy what I'd worked so hard to build up over hundreds, no *thousands* of hours of practice.

Everyone in the sanctuary is looking at me, waiting for me to explain myself.

"I need these calluses," I say. "To play."

Patty suddenly shows a slight interest in me.

"Violin?"

"Ukulele."

This is the wrong answer.

"Baby guitar." Patty sniffs dismissively. "Not a real instrument."

The first month or two of playing ukulele was so so so painful. The strings felt like blades on my tender fingertips. It takes practice, persistence, and patience to improve, three qualities Mom and Lauren say I have in short supply. But even they were impressed when I pushed through the pain to get better. Players have to put up with blistering and bleeding, which is pretty punk rock, right? So it's always annoying when haters like Patty don't give the ukulele any respect.

I'm shocked when Morgan rises to my defense. I thought she might be too annoyed with me to make the effort.

"Actually, Patty," says Morgan. "Ukulele is the fifth most popular music category across all social media platforms. It's not *too* popular, like lip synchs, or not popular enough, like beatboxing. It's the perfect amount of popular."

"I didn't know that," I say.

"I know these things so you don't have to," Morgan says.

It's more accurate to say Maddy researches these things so Morgan doesn't have to. And it sounds like Morgan asked

Maddy to really look into these other categories. Like, how close had Morgan come to choosing Harumi? Everyone knows she's the best beatboxer in our grade. Boys included. Would Harumi be here instead of me if it had ranked just a little higher on the list? Would Harumi be having a better time than I am right now?

"I can't do the manicure without soaking," Patty says.

"I can't play ukulele without calluses," I say.

"Ummm," Morgan says. "This is a problem."

"No!" insists the PA massaging her feet. "There are no problems at Namaste. Only bliss. We'll consult our hand specialist."

"That's not necessary!" I protest as all four PAs exit.

"Let them," Morgan insists. "This is why Namaste is the best."

"But a hand specialist? This isn't major surgery! It's just a stupid manicure that's already caused more trouble than it's worth, because I don't even need it!"

Morgan leans forward in her chair to make a very important point.

"Manicures are not stupid," she says, "and you need one."

The PAs reenter the room with a new fifth member taking the lead. The woman in front introduces herself.

"I'm Amy," she says, "the hand specialist."

Amy is definitely older than the other PAs. She's got lines around her eyes and mouth, but her hands are flawless. When she takes mine in hers it's like being cradled by a baby bunny wrapped in cashmere spun from cumulus clouds, which are the puffiest kind. I don't have Morgan's recall when it comes to, like, percents and stuff, but that's one of the few facts from third-grade science I've actually managed not to forget.

The point is, if Amy is not a hand expert, there are no hand experts.

"You know the international pop superstar Riley Quick?" Amy asks.

"What a question!" Morgan laughs. "She's *only* the most followed person on the internet!"

Riley Quick is also the reason I started playing ukulele. Her solo on "Red Lips, Black Heart" was 100 percent responsible for the sudden surge in ukulele playing among eight-to-eighteen-year-old girls. That's why my mom bought the absolute cheapest one she could find for my tenth birthday, a second-hand soprano for less than ten dollars on eBay, shipping included. She thought my interest in the instrument was just another one of my phases. And maybe it would've been, too, if I hadn't been surprised to discover that I could actually produce a pretty good sound out of a cheap piece of plastic. I picked up the chords and strumming patterns just by watching YouTube tutorials—no private lessons necessary.

So I have no idea what Riley Quick has to do with my calluses until Amy whispers something I obviously mishear because there's no way she said what she just said.

"What?"

And Amy smiles serenely and repeats what she said the first time.

"I do her nails."

That's what I thought she said. And before Morgan can tell her to prove it, Amy holds up her phone to show off a photo of herself being hugged by one of the most famous pop stars in the entire universe.

"OMIGODDESS! OMIGODDESS! OMIGODDESS!"

I sure hope this room is soundproof. Otherwise, I've totally trashed the Zen vibe for everyone within a mile of these four walls.

Fortunately, I'm not the only one losing my mind. Amy tries to explain that before Riley Quick became one of the most famous pop stars in the entire universe, Riley Quick was just a normal girl growing up in Pebble Harbor, New Jersey, and Riley Quick would tag along with Mama Quick when she got her nails done by Amy at this total nothing of a strip mall salon, and I guess Riley and Mama Quick helped Amy get the job at Namaste, and Riley and Mama Quick request her services whenever Riley Quick returns to New Jersey, but really, most of the details of the story are getting totally lost because Morgan and I are too busy freaking out.

"OMIGODDESS!" Morgan shouts.

"OMIGODDESS!" I shout.

"OMIGODDESS!" we shout.

It's all we can say. It takes a lot to impress Morgan, but meeting Riley Quick's hand specialist is one of those things. Morgan has leapt from her chair, and we are literally jumping up and down with joy. She knows how much Riley Quick means to me, and she made this happen. In this moment, I can forget all the awkwardness leading up to right now. I'm grateful to be Morgan Middleton's plus-one. I would never, ever be in this position to get a manicure from Riley Quick's personal aesthetician if it weren't for her.

Morgan abruptly stops jumping and pulls out her phone.

"Our fans are gonna love this!"

She may be happy for me. But she's beyond thrilled for Morgan & Ella.

PRETTY PETTY PLEASE

MORGAN HAS ALREADY CHANGED IN AND OUT OF three different looks since we got to Morgan & Ella HQ. The first was a no-makeup makeup tribute to the end of summer: #BeachyGirlboss. The second—#GlammyGirlboss—was a more dramatic look that required a different shadow for each of the eight separate parts of the eyelid. Morgan could write a series of books even more epic than the Dragonologist Chronicles about the eight separate parts of the eyelid.

#GirlyGirlboss is the third and final look that lands somewhere in between.

"Minimalist, with a bright lip," Morgan explains. "It's, like, a better thematic fit for the song."

She puckers for the mirror. Now that she's done primping and perfecting her aesthetic, she's starting to lose her patience with me.

"Are you ready yet?"

Morgan wants us to record Riley Quick's new single tonight. It dropped yesterday, and I hadn't even heard of it until Morgan told me it was the one we were doing. "Pretty Petty Please" is so new that there aren't reliable ukulele tabs to copy. It was much easier to cover Riley Quick's songs when she was in her ukulele phase, but now she's experimenting with weirder electronic stuff. Some critics say she trying too hard to outdo her nemesis Kaytee K., and as I struggle to translate these bizarre bleep-blorps into chords, I kind of have to agree.

"Almost," I say.

I'm close to having it worked out, but I'll need to listen again to make sure. I put on headphones, press play on the laptop, and turn up the volume to drown out the sound of Morgan's exasperated sighs. "Pretty Petty Please" has gotten thirty million views in less than twenty-four hours, and I'm pretty sure I'm responsible for at least half of them at this point. I remind myself that there was once a time in Riley Quick's career when ten thousand followers was a big deal for her too.

The door to Morgan & Ella HQ bursts open. It's Maddy in zero-chill mode.

"Omigoddess!" she gushes. "Lemme see! Lemme see! Lemme see!"

I hold up my nails, and Maddy almost faints.

"Hashtag Riley Quick Hashtag Ukulele Life Hashtag Asymmetrical Hashtag Namaste Hashtag Mani!"

Amy left my calluses alone. The nails on my right hand are

still longer than my left, but Amy squared them off and applied a shimmery silver lacquer that resists cracking under pressure. I wish the polish worked on, like, a psychological level. Because I'm not sure I can live up to Morgan & Ella's expectations right now.

"The socials are going bonkers!" Maddy raves. "You got, like, two hundred twenty-three new followers just from posting pics. You'll get so many more after you post the video!"

"*If* we ever get around to posting the video," Morgan says. "Ella is taking forehhhhhhhhhhhhhver."

I've been at it for about an hour. I think I've got the chords and strumming patterns pretty much figured out, but that doesn't mean I've mastered performing it. And I obviously can't say it out loud, but my #RileyQuick #UkuleleLife #Asymmetrical #Namaste #Mani isn't making it any easier to play. Amy may have perfected this nail design to keep up with Riley Quick's brutal tour schedule, but I'm not sure it's right for me. Not bad, necessarily. Just different. My nails feel . . . thicker, maybe? Whatever it is, I'm just way too conscious of what's happening with my fingertips. And that hyperawareness is making it kind of impossible to stop playing *notes* and start playing *music*. But I won't know for sure until I try.

"Okay," I say, "let's try to run through it."

So we do. And I must say that it's going well until we reach the chorus.

Pretty petty
Please

(Yeah!)
Get down on your
knees
Pretty petty
Please
(Nah!)
Won't accept your
apologies

Morgan can't hit the whistle note on "apologies." After three attempts, her voice is still cracking.

"Uggggggggh!" Morgan growls. "It's impossible!"

Maddy massages her shoulders, and Morgan shakes her off.

"Riley Quick only hits that note with help from auto-tune."

I know—and dread—what's coming next.

"Let's lower it, Ella."

Morgan doesn't play any instruments. So I can't expect her to understand why this isn't so simple. It's way easier to sing in a different, lower key than it is to transpose a whole song for the ukulele right on the spot just because Morgan can't hit the highest notes on the chorus. Whenever I try to point something like this out to her, she gets mad and reminds me that she has perfect pitch and accuses me of disrespecting vocal music as an art form. But it's not like I don't understand the challenges of singing, because I sing too! *While* I'm playing! And always the lower harmonies even though I'm not an alto! I've always been assigned to the soprano section in every choir I've ever sung in and could probably hit the "apologies" if only Morgan let me try . . .

But.

We are our most harmonious when I just do what Morgan says.

"Okay," I say. "Give me a few minutes . . ."

"A few minutes!" Morgan huffs. "I've already given you forehhhhhhhhver!"

Maddy steps between us and does what she does second best after hashtagging.

"Morgan! Let's record bonus content while Ella works on the song . . ."

Morgan smooshes her lips together in an exaggerated pout.

"I've been telling Ella all summer that we need to post more often." Morgan's mood is already brightening. "I'll need a totally different look."

"Totally!"

As Morgan sashays to her walk-in closet, Maddy gives me the quickest little wink, like the two of us are in this together. But she only dares to make such a gesture behind Morgan's back.

What face does Maddy make when I can't see her?

DISCONNECTION

IT'S THE LAST DAY OF SUMMER BEFORE MY FIRST
day at Mercer Middle School.

Mom is reviewing the back-to-school supplies checklist.

"Backpack? Check. Binders and binder dividers? Check and
check."

I'm only half listening. I'm too busy thinking about following through on tomorrow's Must-Dos. Until I find my
phone, Morgan has reluctantly agreed to deliver these daily
instructions the old-skool way: on paper.

"Highlighters? Number two pencils? Pens? Check. Check.
Check."

One advantage to this new system is that I'll have more
time to make sure I'm following her directions just right.
Morgan will give me tomorrow's Must-Dos today, and the day
after's Must-Dos tomorrow, and so on and so on until I find

my phone and we can go back to sending and getting them by text.

"Ella!"

Judging by Mom's volume, I must not have heard her first two attempts at getting my attention.

"Where is your daily planner?" she asks.

Daily planner? Is this Mom's awkward attempt at a snarky nickname?

"Morgan's at soccer practice or dance class or the equestrian center," I answer.

Mom places both hands on her hips.

"I'm referring to the notebook for writing down homework assignments?"

Ohhhh. *That* daily planner.

"I know I bought you one, because the purple polka-dot planner you *had to have* cost ten dollars more than the plain black one . . ."

The purple polka-dot planner is the same brand Riley Quick uses to write her song lyrics, so totally worth the extra ten dollars, but now is definitely not the time to share this information with Mom because the bottom line is this:

I have no idea where it is.

"I swear I haven't seen it since we left the store . . ." I say.

Mom throws back her head and laughs, but not in a happy way. It's a fed-up *I-can't-believe-this* laugh.

"Ella Jane Plaza! How is it possible that you lost your organizer before school even starts?"

I shrug because I honestly don't know the answer.

"I suppose it's in the same black hole as your phone, all those library books we had to pay fines on, your gym uniform . . ."

"Maybe?"

What else can I say?

"Your disorganization is getting expensive, Ella," Mom says tersely.

My lip quivers, and it gets all fuzzy behind my eyes.

Mom's face changes too. Softens. She sighs in resignation.

"Here's ten dollars," she says, handing me a bill. "You will get on your bike, go to the drugstore, buy the plain black one, and bring back the change . . ."

"Mom! I don't have time for this! Morgan and I are . . ."

"*You* don't have time for this?" Mom points at the clock on the microwave. "I'm going to be late to work!"

"So I can hang out with Morgan afterward."

It's definitely more of a statement of fact than a question. I've watched Morgan do this to get her way, but it doesn't work for me. Not on Mom anyway.

"Not today, Ella," Mom says. "You need to spend this day getting focused. Getting your priorities in order."

"But, Moooooom!" I protest. "Getting my priorities in order is the whole point of hanging out with Morgan today!"

Mom pinches the air in front of her lips. The zip-it gesture means just that.

"We're done here," she says.

She reminds me about the cold cuts I can have for lunch and the frozen burrito and salad I can have for dinner. She reminds me to lock the door behind me and not to open it up for anyone. She reminds me of the neighbors I can go to in case of an emergency. She reminds me that she will be home by seven p.m. She reminds me that when she gets her degree, she should have better job security and more flexibility. She reminds me that she loves me.

Then I watch her go.

Morgan won't like this turn of events. As much as I dread telling her, I know she'll be madder at me if I wait too long to deliver the bad news. I pick up the landline and suddenly realize I don't know what digits to dial. I have no idea what Morgan's phone number is and even less of a clue of how I'd go about getting it.

Now, *this* is a disaster.

Aside from my mom's and Lauren's, there's only one phone number I know by heart. I must have dialed it a millionbilliontrillion times between kindergarten and sixth grade, and I bet it still works now. She's probably the last girl in our grade without her own cell phone. Her parents are even more overprotective than Mom and there are *two* of them.

I bet your mom would let me come over today, says The Best Friend in My Head. *Just like we used to spend every last day of summer together.*

I ignore her, trying not to panic. There has to be a solution to this problem . . . I just have to figure out what it is . . .

Izzy!

I yank open the kitchen drawer closest to the phone, and because there's *a place for everything and everything in its place* . . . I find it! Mom's notepad full of phone numbers and addresses. I often make fun of Mom for not trusting technology, but I'm so grateful for her old fogy ways right now. I find Izzy's info under *I* because I didn't know her last name when Mom asked for it. As I dial the digits, I hope Izzy actually picks up the unrecognized number, because I'm pretty sure Mom has only called her from her own cell phone.

"Hello?"

I'm flooded with relief. "Izzy! It's me! Ella!"

"Ella! Morgan has been asking about you all morning . . ."

I wince at the thought of how losing my phone *and* my notebook has made Izzy's morning more complicated than necessary.

"That's why I'm calling. Could you put Morgan on the phone?"

After a few seconds of muffled voices, Morgan is on the line.

"Ummm, who is this?"

I'm 99.9 percent sure Izzy wouldn't have passed the phone to Morgan without telling her who was calling. And I'm 101 percent sure Morgan wouldn't have picked up otherwise. But this is the kind of harmless drama making that's easier to just go along with than resist.

"It's me," I say. "Ella."

"Ella! Omigoddess! What number is this? Did you get a

new phone? Wait! If you've got a new phone why didn't you just text me?"

"I didn't get a new phone," I say. "This is my landline."

"Your *landline*!" Morgan cracks up. "People still have those?"

"We do," I say. "For emergencies."

"This is an *emergency*?"

She sounds more excited than scared.

"Well"—I hesitate—"sort of . . ."

And that's enough to get Morgan's drama-making imagination going.

"Omigoddess! Did you get a zit? Did you get bangs even though I told you not to? Did you overpluck your eyebrows?" She pauses only to catch her breath. *"Did you chip your manicure?"*

"No, no, no!" I check my hands just to make sure. "And the manicure is still flawless!"

Morgan heaves a heavy sigh of relief. "Then what's the emergency?"

"I can't hang out today."

"Whhhhhhhhhhhattt?" Morgan wails. "But! The! Must! Dos!"

"I know! My mom says I have to stay home and get my priorities in order."

"Duhhhhhh! The Must-Dos are all about getting your priorities in order!"

"That's what I said! But my mom doesn't see it the same way."

"Your mom is so unfair!" Morgan says. "She's not even thinking about how this is affecting *me*!"

Morgan only settles down when I agree to review her Must-Dos one by one, a process that would be so much easier if I hadn't lost my phone. You can't send pics on a landline.

"Okay," I say. "So let's start with my hair . . ."

For the next hour, I describe my hair, makeup, and outfit down to the teensiest detail. Never mind that Morgan already picked out every last millimeter of my #FirstDayLook. At this crucial stage of influence, Morgan & Ella can leave nothing to chance.

"Remember! It's the peace-sign top with the sequins that I gave you and . . ."

"I remember!"

At last, she seems satisfied.

"I *think* we'll be okay," she says. "Just make sure to be at the flagpole no later than seven forty-five so we can make our grand entrance together."

Together. We are in this together. I will not be lost, left out, alone, or loserish. My best friend, Morgan Middleton, won't allow it.

"Maddy will film everything for the socials."

Sometimes I get exhausted by all of Morgan's prep work. But today I'm exhilarated by it. I'm ready to take on Mercer Middle School and the world!

"Hey, by the way, how's the 'Pretty Petty Please' cover doing?" I ask.

I haven't seen any stats on the video since it went live on Morgan & Ella last night. After working so hard to learn the chords and then relearn them in the lower key, I sure hope our fans are rewarding our efforts with lots and lots of love.

"I took it down," Morgan says like no biggie. "It just wasn't *connecting*."

I'm stunned. Less than twenty-four hours ago, Morgan was obsessed with posting that video. And she's already taken it down?

"But it wasn't even up for a whole day! That's not enough time . . ."

"Ummm . . . I've got, like, a gift for knowing what works for us and what doesn't," Morgan says. "If it weren't for my expertise, you'd still be singing in school talent shows with Ickface."

I flinch when she uses the nickname for The Best Friend in My Head, the girl whose phone number I can't forget, no matter how hard over the past year I've tried. It's an old, cold roast Morgan hasn't used all summer, coined in sixth-grade music class because Sophie was just a little too expressive when she sang. Does this mean Sophie's elementary school nickname is back in fiery rotation for middle school? I hope not. But it's not like I can do anything to stop her if it is.

"I guess so . . ."

And it's when Morgan doesn't insist *most definitely so* that I realize she's not even on the line anymore.

READY OR NOT

OUR CALL HAS CUT OUT WITHOUT A GOODBYE.
That's not uncommon—Morgan is always griping about our
town's poor cell coverage—but it feels personal. I stare at the
phone in my hand for a minute or so, trying to make sense of
Morgan's decision to take down the video. When it rings, I
immediately press talk, eager for a do-over.

"Morgan!"

"No, Lala!"

"Lolo!"

I don't know why I'm so surprised to hear my sister's voice.
She's literally one of only two people who have this number.
This is the most action this landline has seen in years. Mom
must have told her I lost my phone.

"Are you ready for the first day of middle school?"

It's just like my sister to get right to it. Lauren hates small talk. College hasn't changed her too much yet.

"I guess so," I say. "How do you know if you're ready?"

"You make plans," she says. "You get organized. You prepare."

"I got a manicure."

"That's not the same thing," Lauren says. "How is a manicure going to help you get into college?"

"But it's, like, a really special manicure," I try to explain. "The nails are shorter on my right hand and longer on my left for—"

Lauren sighs. "You're obviously still hanging around that Morgan girl."

"You've only been gone for a few weeks!" I say. "Of course I'm still hanging out with Morgan. She's my best friend!"

Lauren snorts. She does not like Morgan, but she also doesn't spend a lot of time thinking about her. Not enough to make her Bottom Five, my sister's ever-changing list of The Worst People in the World.

"Have you heard from our father?"

He's always referred to as "our father" by Lauren and "your father" by Mom. The space behind my eyes gets all prickly every time they do. Which, thankfully, isn't all that often. "Our father" battles for the number one spot in Lauren's Bottom Five with a professional soccer player named Luis Somethingsomething, who she really, really hates for reasons I can't remember right now.

"No," I say. "Why would I?"

"He had the nerve to text me right after I got down here," she says. "Sent a picture of himself with the deck crew on a charter somewhere off the coast of Croatia, I think."

I remind myself to find and cross off Croatia on my Secret Map.

"Anyway, he wanted to wish me well in this new stage of my life." Lauren's voice drips with sarcasm. "I thought he might do the same for you."

My throat shrinks.

"No," I croak. "He didn't."

Or if he had, I wouldn't know because I don't have my phone.

"Well, lucky you, then," Lauren says. "I told him to keep his well wishes unless they can help pay my tuition."

"But I thought you didn't want him helping you. I thought you didn't want his money because it gives him power over you. I thought you, um, valued personal freedom over material goods and that transactional relationships are a form of slavery."

Lauren delivered this speech many, many times over the years. I have the whole monologue memorized, even the parts I don't understand.

"I don't want anything from him, but any money would help make Mom's life easier," she says. "It's also the principle of the thing."

Lauren is frequently getting worked up over "the principle of the thing."

Lauren tells me about how much harder soccer practice is in college, tougher than any workouts she's ever gutted through in her whole life. On the upside, her classes so far are actually easier, a benefit of going to one of the best public high schools in the country.

"You should take full advantage of your educational opportunities . . ."

"Uh-huh," I say. "Sure."

She can totally tell that my mind is halfway around the globe, because she wraps up the conversation with classic Lolo efficiency.

"Be good, okay?"

"I'll try."

And whenever Lauren forces me to make that promise—which is often—I always mean it.

I hang up the phone, go to my room, and remove my Secret Map I keep hidden under my mattress. I've only shown this map to one other person, and even then only because she was so much better at geography than I was. From Antigua to Zanzibar, she always found all our father's destinations faster than I ever could.

You also knew I'd keep your map a secret, says The Best Friend in My Head.

Okay. Yeah. For that reason too.

I don't remember our father, which is why I don't miss him like Lauren does. According to her, our father wasn't ready to be married with two daughters. He needed to see what the whole world had to offer while he was still young enough to appreciate it. According to my map, he's been sailing at least three out of the five oceans ever since.

I find Croatia. It's opposite Italy's boot, across the Adriatic Sea. I uncap my Sharpie and mark it with an X. Maybe when I've crossed off enough countries, our father will come back to Mercer, New Jersey, where my sister believes he belongs.

PART TWO

IMAGINARY AUDIENCE

I WAKE UP AN HOUR BEFORE MY ALARM.

MIDDLE SCHOOL!!!

I silently narrate my way through the morning, following a script that's all in my mind for an audience that's only in my imagination.

Hey, guys!

Morgan is filming a real video right at this very second. Apparently September is a bad month for traffic because even our biggest fans have less time to spend on the socials. But Maddy says back-to-school videos are the exception and can still get a lot of attention, so it's important to get them just right. If I hadn't lost my phone, I'd make a video too. Instead, I pretend.

It's my first day of middle school, and I'm superexcited for you all to get ready with me!

I sit up, muss my hair, and mug like the Goofball Goddess I'm supposed to be.

So . . . this is me when I just get out of bed looking like a zombie, but at least I'm still rocking my Riley Quick manicure!

This video would be hashtagged something like Middle School Morning Routine.

So . . . this is me eating a semi-nutritious breakfast of Bran Flakes and Cinnamon Toast Crunch, because vitamins are important but yumminess is too!

No, wait. Back to School Beauty is way better.

So . . . this is me brushing with a whitening toothpaste that tastes gross, but a winning smile is totally worth it, right?

So . . . this is me with my straightener turned up to, like, 450 degrees, but watch out so you don't burn all your hair off!

So . . . this is me putting concealer under my eyes, on my nose, and on the bottom of my chin, but not too much because you don't want to look fake!

First Day Fashion, maybe?

So . . . this is me wearing a sparkly peace-sign tee and dark skinny jeans, and this is totally not spon con, but I wish it was. Hey, Forever 21, hook me up with some swag!

It's so hard for me to know what title would get the most loves, but Maddy's research says our fans like videos that are "interactive and instructional" when we are at our most "approachable and aspirational." Fortunately, the pressure is off because this video only exists in my mind. But for some weird reason, pretending it's real helps me stay focused. Thanks to

Morgan's Must-Dos, I'm good to go in half the time it usually takes me to get ready for school. She's eliminated all the time-sucking *what ifs?* and *is this betters?*

Mom is impressed by my punctuality.

"You're off to a great start!" She beams as she hands over my lunch tote. "May the rest of our mornings be as stress-free as the first!"

I used to show up late to Shadybrook Elementary quite a bit. For months, Mom had no idea because she left earlier than I did. It wasn't until she got called in to discuss my "excessive tardiness" with the vice principal that she became aware of the problem. From that point on, it became Lauren's job to make sure I showed up on time. Personally escorting me to school meant my cranky, sleep-deprived sister had to wake up a half hour earlier than she would have otherwise needed to.

"Why is your irresponsibility my inconvenience?" she'd ask.

Well, I bet she's happy to be in North Carolina and not inconvenienced anymore.

Our apartment isn't far from any of the schools. It's a one-minute drive, a four-minute bike ride, or an eight-minute walk to Shadybrook Elementary. I know this because Sophie timed the route two summers ago. It was her idea, not mine. She was always way more stressed out about my tardies than I ever was. Mercer Middle School is located a few blocks closer than the elementary school, so it should take me even less time to get there.

If you know exactly when you need to leave, says The Best Friend in My Head, *just leave no later than that.*

Well, no duh. Mom and Lauren would call that "a time for everything and everything in its time." But I've got enough motivation without Sophie's know-it-all assistance. I cannot be late for my meet-up with Morgan and Maddy, and I'm not taking any chances. By seven thirty, I'm headed for the door.

"Bye, Mom!" I sling my backpack over my shoulder.

"Oh, no you don't!" She grabs a strap to pull me back. "I'm not letting you go without documenting the occasion!"

I roll my eyes at her. *"Mooooooooom."*

Mooooooooom is not having any of my nonsense. She rolls not only her eyes but her whole head and neck to make sure I understand just how much she is *not having it*. Mom's eye roll is the only one that comes close to giving The Eyeroll any competition.

"You posted a million pictures of yourself this summer," Mom says, reaching for her phone. "You can pose for *one* first-day-of-school photo for your mother."

Mom's exaggerating. I didn't post a *million* pics of myself. I—or, to be more accurate, *Morgan & Ella*—posted about 350 pics to our profiles between the end of June and beginning of September. Maddy's research says five photos a day is "optimal for growth and engagement." I can count on one hand how many of those pics are me solo without Morgan, Maddy, or our fans filling out the frame.

Maybe that's why I'm posing so awkwardly right now. It's like I've never been in front of a camera before.

"Come on, Ella," Mom says. "Loosen up. You can do better for me than that."

Without Morgan, I have no idea what to do with my hands.

IN-BETWEENER

I SHOW UP TO SCHOOL TEN MINUTES BEFORE I'M supposed to meet Morgan and Maddy. This has never happened before.

At least I'm not the only one eager to get this year started. The parking lot is buzzing with busloads of seventh and eighth graders shrieking and shouting . . .

"I MISSED YOU!"

"YO! WHERE YOU BEEN AT?"

Yelling and yelping . . .

"SHUT UP! I DO NOT!"

"DID YOU SEE HIM?"

And basically making way too much noise this early in the morning.

Everyone is asking,

"WHAT HOUSE?"

"WHAT HOUSE?"

"WHAT HOUSE?"

Mercer Middle School divides every grade into two Houses. Students are randomly put in one or the other, so it's not like the Dragonologist Chronicles where the magical Cauldron of Serpentyne sorts clans by disposition. Otherwise my school would be forced to create a Half House to deal with me. I've taken the Official Dragonologist Sorting Quiz a dozen times, and I always fall short of totally belonging anywhere. I'm not a FlusterWing or a FlutterFlame. I'm a FlusterFlutter. A mixed-up in-betweener.

I'll only have academic classes with the students in my own House, taught by our own set of teachers. Because all House One classrooms are on the first floor and all House Two classrooms are on the second floor, my contact with students in the other House is pretty much limited to lunch and gym, and before and after school. Luckily, Morgan, Maddy, and I are all in House One.

"Of course we are," said Morgan the morning in mid-August when we got our assignment letters. "House One is the Cool House. And who is cooler than us?"

Everyone at Mercer Middle School knows House One is the Cool House. When someone asks what house you're in and you answer, "House One," the response is, "Oooh, lucky! That's the Cool House." If you answer, "House Two," the response is, "Oh, too bad. Maybe you can switch?"

I overhear this conversation at least ten times this morning as I lap the lawn, trying to look totally chill. The longer I'm alone, the harder this is.

We could have walked to school together, says The Best Friend in My Head.

And leave myself open to Morgan's ridicule? I don't think so. Showing up on the first day of seventh grade alongside Sophie would be worse for my image than swapping the Must-Dos for a Dragonologist Chronicles T-shirt accessorized with a sack of dragon poop.

But there's also no way I'm standing by the flagpole all by myself with so many seventh and eighth graders watching me, judging me, wondering why this dorky girl is standing all by herself at the flagpole. If I had my phone, I could text Morgan and Maddy or light up Fotobomb or just pretend to do those things if I didn't actually feel like doing those things. It's so much harder to look like you've got friends when you don't have a phone.

"You!"

A cheery girl in double buns and a Riley Quick tee is pointing right at me.

"Omigoddess!" She grabs my hand. "Your manicure is even more perfect in person!" She snaps a quick picture of my nails. "Where's Morgan?" And before I can answer she throws her arm around me and pulls me in for a selfie. I've never seen her before in my life, but she has seen me. Many, many times.

"I love your videos!"

She's not looking at me. She's focused on her phone as she edits and enhances the pics before posting.

"Please, please, please tag me!" she pleads. "A shout-out from Morgan & Ella would mean everything to me!"

"Well . . . okay . . . but . . ."

I don't even know this girl's name, and there's no time to ask because she squeals and dashes off. I guess she assumes I'll find out anything I need to know about her on the socials? The whole interaction takes less than five seconds, but it's long enough to catch Morgan's attention.

"Too busy posing to meet us at the flagpole?"

"Whew!" I spin around and hug her. "I'm so relieved you're here!"

She holds her arms stiffly at her sides.

"Seriously, are my directions too hard to follow?"

I'm wearing the outfit she told me to wear. I put on the makeup she told me to put on. I straightened my hair the way she told me to straighten it. Is she really mad because I'm not at the flagpole? And what does it matter when we're all together now on the sidewalk?

"Morgan, it's 7:44! I'm still early! And we're all here!"

Maddy listens in silence, waiting to see how Morgan responds. I get an exaggerated winky emoji face and a shove.

"Omigoddess! I'm just kidding!"

And she laughs, and Maddy laughs, so I laugh too.

"It's just too bad for her that you didn't wait, like, another five seconds, because she could have posed with *both* of us and gotten way more loves," Morgan says. "I mean, who is Ella without Morgan, am I right?"

She is right.

"Let's give the Oh-Em-Gees what they really want!" Maddy suggests.

"The *what*?" I ask.

"Not what! Who!"

"Who *who*?"

Morgan and Maddy laugh.

"Who do you think? Duh! Our fans!" Morgan says. "The Omigoddesses! The Oh-Em-Gees!"

This news takes me by surprise. I mean, just four days ago Morgan was annoyed because I wasn't brainstorming ideas. And now the decision has been made without asking how I felt about it first?

Morgan makes a hand heart to match her sequined LOVE T-shirt.

"When was that decided?" I ask.

"I dunno. Yesterday?" Morgan shrugs.

"It was, like, crucial to get done before the launch of your back-to-school socials," Maddy adds, holding up her phone.

"Come on, Ella." Morgan knocks her shoulder into mine. "Make peace."

Isn't that what I'm doing by not complaining about being totally left out of a major decision for Morgan & Ella?

"Ella," Morgan repeats in a sharper tone. *"Peace."*

It takes a moment to understand what Morgan really means. She wants the pose to match my T-shirt. I lift my hands, make a V with two fingers, and smile.

clickclickclickclickclickclickclickclickclick

#GoalzGirlz #Omigoddesses #OMGs #FirstDayFierceness

clickclickclickclickclickclickclickclickclick

#Love #Peace

Morgan links her arm in mine. "Let's do this thing!"

Morgan & Ella march to the front of Mercer Middle School, every step of the grand entrance captured by Maddy for the OMGs.

cliquecliquecliquecliquecliquecliqueclique

FOTOBOMBED!

IT'S A GOOD THING WE AGREED TO MEET UP FIFTEEN minutes before the homeroom bell. We're not making much progress down the hall, because we're stopped every few seconds.

"I MISSED YOU!"

"YO! WHERE YOU BEEN AT?"

The "noise" isn't as annoying when I'm a part of it.

"SHUT UP! I DO NOT!"

"DID YOU SEE HIM?"

It's comforting to be greeted so enthusiastically by familiar faces from Shadybrook Elementary. I know Morgan is super-social, but I'm still surprised when she's high-fived by an eighth grader from the travel soccer team, hugged by a girl from her equestrian center, and asked "What house?" by a boy from her hip-hop class wearing way too much body spray.

Every time I'm on the verge of lost, left-out, alone loserdom, Morgan takes a moment to introduce me to her friends.

"Brianna! This is Ella! The Goofball Goddess! She's the best!"

"Hailey! This is Ella! The Goofball Goddess! She's the best!"

"Jonah! This is Ella! The Goofball Goddess! She's the best!"

I stick out my tongue. I suck in my cheeks. I cross my eyes.

I play along because it is so much safer on the inside of Morgan's circle than outside of it. Though I kind of wish that maybe Morgan would say something a little more specific about why I'm the best. Like, maybe mention my ukulele skills or something more flattering than goofballing. But I'm grateful for the intros, because Morgan doesn't even acknowledge Maddy's existence as she records it all for the socials. She's grinning wider than the emoji on her HAPPY T-shirt, so I guess Maddy doesn't mind? After all, she always says "act as if I'm not here!" when she's recording us.

"I toooooold you." Morgan posts the latest round of pics. "We're the most popular girls in seventh grade, and we haven't even gotten to homeroom yet."

And to be honest, I'm not really in a hurry to get there. Homerooms are alphabetical. *Middleton, Morgan* and *Monroe, Madeline* are lucky enough to be grouped together in Room 115. *Plaza, Ella* is located right across the hall in 116, but it sort of feels like I'm headed for Croatia or any of the other faraway destinations on my Secret Map. By the time we reunite after our ten-minute homeroom, Morgan and Maddy will have compared schedules. I'll already be behind and need catching up.

So I'm sort of feeling sorry for myself again when Morgan reminds me that my situation could be so much worse.

"Check out your Beeeeee Effffffff Effffffffffff."

She points a finger and elongates every letter for maximum mortifying impact. I know she's referring to Sophie before I even spot her down the hall. She's peering intensely at the school map on the wall for who knows what reason, because I know for a fact she's had the floor plan memorized since fifth grade.

"She's not my BFF," I say curtly.

"Are you sure?" Morgan says. "I mean, I would understand if you wanted to quit Morgan & Ella and go back to singing in talent shows with Ickface."

Maddy shudders. "Don't even joke about that!"

Morgan charges toward Sophie, phone up and out.

"FOTOBOMBED! Ugly Outfit of the Day!"

Sophie startles, as if Morgan has pointed a gun at her. Honestly, in Morgan's grip, a phone is just as terrifying.

clickclickclickclickclickclickclickclickclick

I honestly don't know why Morgan is targeting Sophie like this. Her outfit isn't ugly at all. I like it—especially the swirly blue-green T-shirt. I swear I've seen that top in one of my fashion magazines. The print reminds me of a spinning globe.

It reminds Morgan of something else.

"Ummm . . . Sophie? Whole Foods wants its moldy cheese back." She sniffs the air around her. "Stinks like Roquefort too."

Aha! I've figured out where I've seen this shirt before. Last month's *Vogue*! Eco/Echo is a new female-owned company that uses all-natural fabrics and low-impact dyes. Of course Sophie puts the conscience back in fashion consciousness. For all I know, my neon-sequined tee could've been sewn by a toddler in a sweatshop located in a country so small and so far away that I'd never be able to find it on my Secret Map.

None of this is even close to being an okay thing to say.

Instead, I do what I always do when I'm at a loss for what to say and I don't have a script. I fall back on my Goofball Goddessness.

"Ugh. What's a Roquefort?"

"Duh! A moldy cheese that looks exactly like her shirt!"

It all happens so fast. *Too* fast for Sophie to do anything but stare googly-eyed in disbelief. Morgan is already tapping away on her phone, captioning the pic for Fotobomb. It's her favorite of the socials lately, because the posts only last for ten minutes before self-destructing. Followers rush to get in on the explosion of love while they have a chance.

Or—in this case—hate.

Within seconds, Morgan & Ella's followers—the OMGs—sizzle with flaming commentary.

UGLIEST OUTFIT OF THE DAY
MORE LIKE ROACH-FART
FIRST DAY OF SCHOOL FAIL

Why hold back on trolling when everything you say blows

up—kaboom!—and disappears without a trace within ten minutes?

If I know her at all—and I think I still do because Sophie hasn't changed since preschool—she's probably wondering how Morgan and Maddy are so boldly ignoring the school's "no phones" policy that was clearly outlined in the Mercer Middle School student handbook distributed to all incoming seventh graders over the summer. This is exactly the type of rule breaking that makes Sophie all twitchy. She's never cared about her clothes, so I bet this phone violation bothers her even more than the comparison to stinky cheese. She's milliseconds away from quoting the handbook from memory, which will only make Morgan launch even meaner Fotobomb memes. I can't stop Morgan from roasting Sophie, but I don't have to be, like, indirectly responsible for making it worse. I have to create a distraction and fast. So I do it the best way I know how.

"Ugh," I say in my ditsiest voice. "How do you even *spell* 'Roquefort'?"

I'm saying it for Sophie's sake, but she doesn't know that.

She can't even look at me.

I've never seen her so disappointed. And she's had many reasons to be disappointed in me. Even before Morgan came along.

Sophie put together word lists for spelling. She created trivia questions for social studies. She made flashcards for science. And despite all her help, I never got an A. But she never gave up on me. She was always insisting I was just a few words, a few questions, a few flashcards away from totally getting it. And she promised to stick with me until I did.

Because that's what best friends do, says The Best Friend in My Head.

Now this is totally bonkers because Sophie is still standing right in front of me and if I want to talk to her directly, I still can. I can ask a friendly question, the easiest one to ask. And maybe, with that simple gesture, she'll look a little less disappointed in me.

But I don't ask Sophie what House she's in.

And her face doesn't change as she finally gets herself together, takes a wide step around us, and walks away. When she heads for the second-floor stairwell, none of us are surprised.

The Uncool House is where Sophie belongs. And thanks to Fotobomb, there are now OMGs all over the school, the county, the state—maybe even the *country*—who 100 percent agree.

THIS IS ME

THE AUDIENCE IN MY HEAD NEVER STARTS A FLAME
war.

Hey, OMGs! Come follow along with me on my first day of school!

So . . . this is me comparing schedules with Morgan and Maddy after homeroom. And it's, like, half the best and half the worst because their schedules are exactly the same and I've got four periods the same and four periods totally different where we won't get to see one another at all! Don't you hate it when that happens?

But at least we start our day all together! We head into first period language arts, and we know right away we're going to like this class because our teacher, Miss Lee, glows like a Fotobomb beauty guru bathed in halo light, and she's wearing wedge-heeled boots and this edgy moto jacket and has all these inspirational quotes all over the walls like the lines from "The Fullest Truth" that go:

Stop concealing

Revealing is healing

Give me the fullest truth

Hey, should that be our next cover song? Are you into Kaytee K.? Any Kayters out there? Let us know in the comments! Anyway, Miss Lee lets us pick our own seats, so of course Morgan sits next to me and she tells Maddy to sit behind her, and when Miss Lee asks us to share a little something about ourselves, Morgan mentions horseback riding and travel soccer but not Morgan & Ella, which I think is a little weird until Maddy jumps in and says to Miss Lee and the whole class that Morgan is being too humble because Morgan & Ella is exploding on Fotobomb. And that's all thanks to you! The OMGs! We love you guys. We wouldn't be here without you! Anyway, I don't have to say anything, because Maddy has already said it for me so I just smile, smile, smile.

Second period is social studies, and we already know Mrs. Munson won't be as cool as Miss Lee because she's more like a grandma in her lumpy cardigan and sensible shoes, but she also lets us pick our own seats, and this time Morgan sits next to me on one side and she tells Maddy to sit on the other side of her. So we're sitting all in a row, and Mrs. Munson notices our T-shirts. PEACE! HAPPY! LOVE! They remind her of the posters she carried during peaceful hippie protests way back in the 1960s, which just goes to show that no matter how much things change, things stay the same, and this is why it's important to study history, and by the end of class we're thinking maybe

Mrs. Munson isn't so bad. Never judge a person by their lumpy cardigan! She's just a makeover away from coolness!

So now this is when the day takes a turn. Switch to black and white! Cue the saddest music that won't violate copyrights! This is me saying goodbye to Morgan and Maddy as they leave for Mandarin and I head for Spanish class. Adios, mis amigas. I won't see them until lunch. How will I make it through Spanish, math, and science?

Guess what? I'm rescued by an OMG! That's right! That girl in the double buns with the adorable dimples is Paisley. She's the first Morgan & Ella fan I've met at Mercer Middle School, and we have the next three classes together. She's the hint of color in the grayscale. The brief shift from minor to major key. I have a feeling you'll be seeing a lot more of Paisley.

I won't torture you by making you follow me in math or science, because I'd rather fast-forward to lunch.

Lunch! This is me being reunited with Morgan and Maddy, and we hug one another because it feels like a millionbilliontrillion years since I last saw them. Obviously, catching up is our priority number one. Eating is, like, the second most important part of lunch. And Morgan says it's very hard to look cute while chewing, so you don't need to see that. Any foodie followers? Do you want to know what we pack in our lunches? Post in the comments below. We can do a separate video, because this one is already way too long and I still have two periods to go.

After lunch, Morgan, Maddy, and I have a class called Digital Citizenship, and we're pretty psyched because Morgan says the eighth graders on her travel soccer team told her it's all about using the internet, and how fun is that? And it sounds like an easy A, right? But within two seconds we already know we're going to hate it, because Mr. Schlosser makes us sit in alphabetical order, which works out fine for Middleton, Morgan and Monroe, Madeline, but who knew there were so many kids with names starting with Ns and Os? I'm, like, in a totally different row. And also we don't know what those eighth graders were talking about, because this class is definitely not about optimizing our presence on Fotobomb. After listening to Mr. Schlosser drone on for forty minutes we still have no idea what this class is supposed to teach us other than to hate Digital Citizenship.

So . . . this is all of us all sad coming out of Digital Citizenship and me especially because I've got PE eighth period without Morgan and Maddy, but then Morgan makes me feel better by saying last period gym is the best because at least I don't have to worry about messing up my look. So even though I'm leaving Morgan and Maddy again, I'm feeling pretty confident going into the gymnasium, and I walk in, scan the bleachers for a familiar face, and see—

Whoopsie! Technical issues! My bad! You'll never get to see that part of my day. But don't worry, OMGs, you didn't miss anything worth seeing . . .

REMEDIAL GYM

MOM DOESN'T HAVE MUCH TIME TO CHAT ABOUT my first day. So why does she make it even harder by asking all the questions I have zero interest in answering?

"So!" She kicks off her clogs. "Do you like your classes?"

Morgan and Maddy are in my language arts and social studies classes, so those are the best classes. We are in different math and science because they're way smarter than I am. And we're in different foreign language classes because they take Mandarin and I take Spanish. So those classes are terrible classes, but not the worst because Paisley is in them with me.

"Omigoddess!" She squeaked and did a little victory dance when we compared schedules in Spanish, the first of our three classes together. "Hashtag Goalz Girlz!"

Paisley is *intense*. She is very determined to be my BFF even though she doesn't know me. I haven't spent enough time with her to decide if I like her very much, but at least I've got some-one who will always want to sit next to me when Morgan and Maddy aren't around.

Except for in PE.

PE is the worst class of all. And I don't want to think about how awkward and awful it is, but Mom is still waiting for me to say something.

"They're okay."

This answer puts two vertical lines right between Mom's eyes. She should know better than to try again, but she does anyway.

"Do you like your teachers?"

My language arts and social studies teachers are my favorites because they let us pick our own seats, so I get to sit next to Morgan and Maddy, which is majorly important, because as I've already said, I don't see them much even though we're in the same House. Thank goddess we all have lunch at the same time, because Paisley has it next period, and I might have eaten mine in a toilet stall like all the pathetic outcasts in the best teen movies.

"They're okay" is what I say instead.

This answer adds another furrow, turning the 11 into 111. I try to say something positive before the wrinkles multiply into the millionbilliontrillions.

"Morgan & Ella got a ton of new followers on Fotobomb for our back-to-school posts," I say brightly, "and our biggest fans are now officially calling themselves Oh-Em-Gees, which is supercute and—"

I'm silenced by the force of Mom's sigh.

"Do you have anything to say about your first day of school that doesn't revolve around Morgan Middleton?"

I think about her question for a few seconds, which is just long enough for Mom to figure out the answer for herself.

"Ella! You're at school to learn, not to socialize!" She hoists *A Field Guide to Physical Dysfunction* and taps the cover. "If I had focused more and socialized less when I was your age, I wouldn't be working so hard to catch up now!"

She shoves the textbook into her backpack with an irritated groan.

I almost want to laugh.

Mom has no idea just how hard I'm working to be the perfectly imperfect Goofball Goddess Morgan needs me to be.

"Your sister understood the importance of an education," Mom continues. "I wish . . ."

Her voice trails off into the unspoken:

She wishes I were better than not-great at school.

She wishes I weren't so silly and obsessed with the socials.

She wishes I wanted to be more like Lauren and less like Morgan.

"I've got homework to do."

It's not much. As a way of getting to know us, Miss Lee asked us to write a paragraph describing our favorite book and why. I'm struggling to come up with a book that Morgan finds acceptable, which means nothing from the Dragonologist Chronicles. I'll probably pick a pop star's autobiography or a beauty vlogger's how-to. Anyway, it's not like I want to get to work right now, but it's the most acceptable excuse for leaving Mom's bedroom as quickly as possible. It would hurt too much to find out she's too disappointed to kiss me goodbye.

She wishes, says The Best Friend in My Head, *you were still best friends with me.*

There's no way this is going to happen.

Even though the only girl I know in PE is Sophie.

Yes, *that* Sophie.

I think they threw together all the unsportiest girls from both Houses in last period. It's like remedial gym. Sophie and I pretended not to see each other when I dashed into the gymnasium as the final bell rang. To Sophie, early equals punctual and on time is late, so she was already waiting in the stands for class to start. At least she had two other not-sporty girls from Shadybrook Elementary—Harumi and Sofie-with-an-f—to sit next to her.

I was the one who walked all the way up to sit by myself in the back row, not her.

I was the one who looked like a loser, not her.

I was the one who looked like she belonged in the Uncool House, not her.

I'm so glad Morgan wasn't there to witness it.

Then again, when I'm with Morgan it's

clickclickclickclickclick

cliquecliquecliquecliqueclique

and I'm never

lost
alone
left out
loserish
or Uncool.
It was the longest, loneliest forty minutes of my life.

OXYMORONS

MORGAN IS SHOUTING AT ME FROM ACROSS THE bleachers.

"Act natural!"

I'm on my back, stretched across a narrow metal railing, modeling a crop turtleneck and flowy flowered skirt Morgan gave me. Nothing about this reverse plank is natural, but I'm trying to make it look superchill.

"And cute!" Morgan yells at me. "Don't forget to look cute!"

I never forget to look cute—not with Morgan as my personal stylist and shopper. I don't want to sound ungrateful for all the free fashion, but I wish I had a little more input on my looks. This top is a bit choky, and I keep getting all tangled up in this skirt.

"Ella!" Morgan shouts. "We don't have time for this!"

We've only got about fifteen minutes before Morgan meets

up with Brianna for soccer practice. Or is it Hailey? All the popular eighth graders look the same to me. We have to nail the shot so Morgan & Ella can post during the peak hours of three and five p.m. According to Maddy, that's the sweet spot, when all local elementary schools have let out but parents aren't making the littles do their homework yet. The OMGs seem to especially love any posts of us at Mercer Middle School, which is why we're posing in the bleachers next to the athletic fields.

Morgan stops posing long enough to thrust her chin at the group of girls kicking soccer balls across the grass.

"Losers."

Morgan won't play for the Mercer Middle School team because it "isn't competitive enough." Our athletic department has a "no-cuts" policy. Any student who wants to participate can join the team, regardless of skill or experience.

"Why bother playing for a terrible team?"

On the other foot, the Mercer Travel League takes the very best. Morgan is the only seventh grader expected to play with the older girls this season, which is a huge honor, but she won't know for sure until tryouts are over. Players have to earn a spot on the team every year. If she doesn't maintain a certain level of excellence, she's out. She says it's ruthless—just like showbiz— and that's why she likes it.

Morgan redirects her attention my way.

"Ella! You're superawkward, but not in a cute way!"

"Why can't I just pose next to you?"

Morgan is standing above me doing a classic hand-in-pocket/knee-pop combo. So easy.

"Ummm." Morgan ding-dongs her head. "You clearly don't understand anything about achieving the perfect composition in plandids."

"Plandids?"

"Planned candids!" Morgan and Maddy reply simultaneously.

"Planned candids? Isn't that a . . ."

I try to remember the funny word Miss Lee talked about in language arts that means, like, a contradiction in terms.

Jumbo shrimp, for example.

Open secret.

Only choice.

Act natural.

Sophie would know the word I'm searching for.

"Look," Morgan says seriously, "I understand that not having a phone has set you back, like, a zillion centuries."

"She's almost as bad as Mr. Schlosser," Maddy cracks.

"It may not be possible for you to achieve his ultimate level of Digital Citizenship," Morgan says sarcastically, "but can you at least try to keep up with the social media basics?"

I am trying. All I do is try. And when I'm not trying, I'm trying to look like I'm *not* trying. But at least all my hard work in faking effortless cool is paying off. It's only been two weeks, but Morgan says we are definitely the most popular girls in seventh grade, just as she predicted. Paisley was the first of my classmates to beg for a shout-out, but apparently the requests are nonstop on the socials.

UR PERFECT TAG MEEEEEEE

SO JELLY I LOVE YOU PLEEEEASE TAG

GIRLBOSSNESS GOOFBALLNESS GORGEOUSNESS TAG TAG TAG

I say "apparently" because I only see what Morgan and Maddy show me. Otherwise, I'd be totally oblivious to our "popularity." Our Fotobomb profile may be exploding, but I haven't really met anyone new at Mercer besides Paisley, who, honestly, I don't know much about other than her commitment to the Morgan & Ella fandom. Let's see. She rrrrrrrreally rrrrrrrolls herrrrrrrr *rrrrrrrr*s in Spanish class.

"Obvs, Morgan is your BFF," Paisley said on the second day of school, "but I can fill in for her when she's not around!"

So I let her. She sits next to me in class and partners up with me on projects and deals with all the jealous girls who could've been in her position if they were first to post a selfie with me.

"When are you getting a new phone?" Morgan asks now.

She's still standing above me but gazing at the distant clouds in a way that is supposed to look like she's thinking deep thoughts.

"I told you," I say. "My mom won't get me a new phone. She thinks I need to learn to be more responsible . . ."

Morgan pouts.

"You know what's irresponsible? Leaving *me* to make up for your nonexistent social media presence . . ."

To be honest, I think this arrangement is working out pretty well for both of us. Morgan can have total control over our brand, and I can pretend everyone loves it. I know it isn't true because, you know, haters gonna hate. But they rarely—if ever—hate right to your face. This is why Morgan's daily Fotobomb attacks on Sophie are so . . . so . . .

What's the right word to complete that sentence?

A) Bold

B) Brazen

C) Bullying

D) All of the Above

I'm about to remind Morgan how much better she is at Fotobombing than I am when I start wibble-wobbling off the side of the railing. Fortunately the fall happens in sloooooow motion so it's like a very low-impact, butt-first crash to the bottom bleacher.

"OOF."

No major injuries, but I wince in anticipation of the roasting I deserve for messing up the, um, *plandid*.

But Morgan isn't mad. She and Maddy are cracking up.

"Did you get all that, Maddy?"

"Of course! Hashtag Outtakes! Hashtag Bloopers!"

Morgan fist-bumps Maddy, then me. "Classic Goofball Goddess!"

"Whaaaat?" I'm so confused. "You *wanted* me to fall off the railing?"

"Totally!"

I peer down at the drop to the mud if I'd toppled over the opposite side of the railing. It's less than a few feet to fall, but still.

"What if I'd gotten really hurt?"

"You didn't get hurt," Morgan says, picking up her gym bag.

"But what if I did?"

"The OMGs would be *devastated*," Maddy answers. "Hashtag Pray for Ella."

"Why didn't you just tell me you *wanted* me to fall off the railing?"

Morgan's phone buzzes.

"That's Hailey, I gotta go. We got what we needed, and that's why you're the best Goofball ever!"

Morgan gives me a hug and hops off the bleachers.

"Don't forget the Must-Dos!"

I never forget the Must-Dos.

Morgan blows us kisses then dashes across the field to meet up with her soccer friends.

"Morgan's superior time management is what makes her such a Girlboss," Maddy says.

I guess my inferior sense of balance is what makes me such a Goofball?

I rub my butt, wondering how bad the bruise will be.

"We couldn't tell you what we wanted," Maddy explains, "or it wouldn't look spontaneous."

"So you set me up to fall."

"Exactly!" Maddy says, folding up her travel tripod. "Set-up spontaneity!"

Set-up spontaneity is another example of that word I can't remember . . .

An oxymoron, says The Best Friend in My Head.

The Best Friend in My Head. Ha. That's an oxymoron too.

FAKE FOLLOWERS

THE OMGS ARE LOVING THE CLIP OF ME FALLING off the railing.

YOU ARE HILAR

SO GORGE

ADORBS

But Morgan is the opposite of happy when I meet up with her before homeroom this morning.

"Are you buying fans?"

This isn't the greeting I expected.

"*What?*"

"Are you," she says slowly, "buying fans on Fotobomb?"

I'm thinking this is a setup for another joke that plays off my Goofball Goddessness. But Maddy isn't recording this conversation, which means this is one of those rare moments meant for real life only.

"Are you serious?"

Her eyes are icy, but her cheeks are ablaze.

"Do I look like I'm not serious?"

Morgan's most intimidating when she runs hot and cold at the same time. I've witnessed this stormy mood many times before—when Maddy inserted herself in a selfie or Izzy picked us up ten minutes late or the Frootie Smoothie barista misspelled her name (MORGON) on a takeaway cup—but never for something *I* did. Not even when I lost my phone.

"You are totally in charge of Fotobomb," I remind her.

"That's why it's so weird," she says. "You're getting all these new followers."

"*We're* getting new followers . . ."

"But *you* are getting more," Morgan says.

"What? Fotobomb doesn't keep track of our individual followers."

"It's a new feature," Maddy explains from over Morgan's shoulder.

Morgan thrusts her phone in my face. It's open to the Morgan & Ella Fotobomb page. In addition to our numbers as a duo (15,002—whoa!), there are tallies under each of our names.

Morgan has 10,006.

I have 10,226.

How is it possible for me to have two hundred more followers than Morgan? I don't blame Morgan for suspecting something shady. I wouldn't believe it myself if the numbers weren't right in front of me.

"Morgan, how can I buy fans? I don't even have a phone! And I wouldn't know how to go about it even if I did!"

"It is a pretty complicated process," says Maddy. "And expensive too."

"That's true," Morgan sniffs. "You don't have enough money to buy any bots."

What she's saying is true. I can't afford to buy fake followers. And while I appreciate being cleared of the accusation, that truth isn't any less hurtful to hear.

"Clearly the algorithm is off," Maddy says. "The programmers will correct it soon, I'm sure."

I have no idea what Maddy is talking about, but I nod vigorously as if I do.

"We're supposed to be equals, Ella," Morgan says. "And this imbalance just makes us look bad as a brand." She turns on her heel and heads to her classroom without another word. Maddy hangs back just long enough to whisper an ominous warning.

"Do. Not. Get. More. Popular. Than. Morgan."

The rest of the day doesn't get much better.

I don't like talking about classes for obvious reasons. The only subject I have *any* success in is social studies, and that's because we're starting with a unit on geography. I'm able to identify a few continents and countries because I recognize them from the Secret Map underneath my mattress.

I get my math test back, and it's no surprise that I've bombed it. Okay, I didn't fail it, but I didn't ace it either. And with perfectionist friends like Morgan and Maddy and a genius sister like Lauren, a C might as well be an F. My math teacher requires parental signatures on all tests, and for the rest of the day I'm dreading showing it to Mom because she's really, really hoping this will be the year I'll get it together grade-wise.

It's not happening.

So I'm totally distracted during our afternoon shoot. And Morgan gets mad at me because I keep messing up the choreography she gave me five minutes to learn. After a few flubbed takes that aren't funny enough in a Goofball Goddess kind of way, she cuts it short.

"Go home, Ella," Morgan says. "You're a *disaster*."

By the time I get to the apartment, I'm totally drained and not in the mood for the lecture I'll get for the math test. If I catch Mom right before she leaves for class, maybe she won't have time to deliver it.

"Hey, Mom," I say as she's reaching for the doorknob. "By the way . . ."

She frowns when she sees the test in one hand and a pen in the other.

"Let me guess," she says. "You need a signature on something you don't want me to see."

She knows what's up. My mom is so much smarter than I give her credit for.

Than many people give her credit for.

"I can't say I'm thrilled about this," Mom says, tapping the red Xes for every incorrect answer. "A C isn't the end of the world, but I think you'll agree it isn't the best start of the school year either."

I nod.

"If I accept a C in September," Mom says, "you'll be failing in June."

I nod.

"You need to get your priorities in order," she continues. "Stop spending so much time on those silly videos and more time on your schoolwork."

I nod.

"Until your grades improve, I want you to come straight home every day after school and do your homework."

This punishment should feel like the end of the world.

But it doesn't.

To be honest, I'm kind of worn out by all the demands of being half a brand. Morgan says I have no reason to complain since she's handling all the socials *and* playing travel soccer *and* horseback riding *and* taking dance classes. And I'm grateful for Paisley and all the other OMGs who, for whatever reason, really, really like us and want more. But I need a little break from being the Goofball Goddess. I kind of understand why Gigi from Fourth Dimension had that epic meltdown after the Grammys.

"Okay," I say. "Fine."

Mom raises her eyebrows.

"That's it?" she says. "No protests? No pleading?"

"Nope," I say. "You're right. I need to take my work more seriously."

She studies me for a moment. Lauren says that when Mom looks at us like that, she's seeing all the way down to our souls.

"If I didn't know any better," Mom says, "I'd think you were happy about this punishment."

It's really impossible to get anything past Mom.

"I don't know what you're talking about," I say.

TOTALLY BLANK

ONE PERSON WHO WILL DEFINITELY NOT BE HAPPY about my punishment is Morgan. And I guess I'm nervous about telling her because I need to pee really, really bad even though I *never* pee at this time of day. I can't remember the last time I actually used a school bathroom to, you know, *go* to the bathroom. Even Lauren is impressed by my bladder—on a normal day I can hold in for like, eight hours, no problem.

But today is not that day.

So I'm in the stall, doing my business, when I hear the door open. Two girls enter in midconversation. I automatically lift my feet so they can't see I'm inside. I know everyone pees but it's, like, still embarrassing.

"I'm just glad Sophie doesn't have a phone," one girl is saying.

"And doesn't see all the horrible stuff posted about her," another girl is saying.

I recognize the voices as Harumi and Sofie-with-an-f. And this already-awkward situation has just gotten worse.

"She can't stop it?" Harumi asks.

"Morgan is unstoppable," Sofie-with-an-f says.

"She's too afraid," Harumi says.

"And I kind of can't blame her," Sofie-with-an-f says. "Isn't that why we aren't doing anything about it?"

"If we stand up for Sophie," Harumi says, "we'll be Chewy and Lickity Lick all over again."

They aren't wrong. Harumi and Sofie-with-an-f both caught Morgan's snarky attention in the past. For all of fifth grade, Harumi was called "Chewy" because she has a habit of biting the ends of her hair. And Sofie-with-an-f was better known as "Lickity Lick" for the slurpy way she runs her tongue over her braces after meals. Fortunately for them, this was before Fotobomb. Sophie hasn't been so lucky.

"How can you be best friends with someone you're afraid of?" Harumi asks.

"That's *why* Morgan picked Ella to be her best friend," Sofie-with-an-f says. "She knows Ella will never call out her bad behavior."

I almost fall into the toilet.

The "she" they're referring to—*She* can't stop it? *She's* too afraid—isn't Sophie.

It's me.

"Ella's too nice to be best friends with Morgan," Harumi says.

My heart lifts a little. They don't think I'm a terrible person after all.

"That's what I used to think," Sofie-with-an-f says. "But Ella isn't nice. She's just, like, blank."

I sag, slipping dangerously low in the bowl.

"Totally blank!" Harumi says with a cackle. "There's nothing there!"

And the door opens again, and their voices are swallowed up by the hallway noise.

I'm all wobbly when I stand up.

Blank.

Totally blank.

Nothing there.

I'd still be paralyzed by those words if not for the alarming drip drip drip of liquid running down my back because— EWWWWWWWW—my brand-new Must-Do shirt is saturated with toilet water.

CHARITABLE BULLYING

I HAVE JUST ENOUGH TIME TO SOAP, RINSE, AND dry my top before Morgan sweeps into the bathroom for my daily twirl. Maddy, as always, is following right behind.

"Omigoddess! So cute today!"

I'm dizzy with relief. Morgan has no idea that just a few minutes ago, I was washing pee water out of the navy-and-white-striped boatneck top she selected for me today. All she sees is that I've followed her Must-Dos down to the last eyelash. My makeup is "subtle sunkiss." I've got a single braid woven into my ponytail, and I'm wearing that top along with the distressed cropped jeans and slip-ons she also gave me.

"Seriously!" Morgan squeezes next to me for a selfie. "Perfection!"

I wish Sofie-with-an-f and Harumi were here to witness this.

See? I'd say. *There* is *something here. I'm* not *totally blank. I'm perfection . . .*

"Omigoddess! Wait until you see the throwback looks I've put together for today's shoot . . ."

Oh no. I've gotten so caught up in Morgan's praise that I've forgotten all about being grounded. This morning has already been stressful and we haven't even gotten to homeroom yet. If I get the disastrous news out of the way, maybe I can bounce back and make the rest of the day a little less terrible than it already is. I decide to come right out with it.

"I'm grounded."

Morgan shivers. Maddy does too, like the shock is contagious.

"Grounded???" Morgan's tone is more like an accusation than a question.

"Grounded," I repeat. "I have to come home straight after school every day."

Morgan huffs. "But we're recording our throwback video this afternoon!"

"I know."

I spent three hours teaching myself a Spice Girls medley on the uke. Not to mention all the harmonies.

"How long are you grounded?" Maddy asks.

"I don't know."

"You didn't negotiate an end date?" Morgan is stunned. "If you can't argue your mother out of grounding, the very least you can do is negotiate the terms of your punishment!"

This is a perfectly logical tactic for the daughter of a lawyer. But my mom has no time for back talk.

"We'll just have to produce more content on the weekends," I suggest.

"Do you have any idea how booked I am on the weekends? I have *obligations*, you know. *Commitments*."

Morgan exhales deeply.

Maddy nods emphatically.

I watch nervously.

"But our brand is a priority," Morgan says. "So I'll have Izzy move some things around if that's what it takes . . ."

And this is my cue to throw my arms around her in gratitude.

"Thank you! Thank you! Thank you!"

Morgan smiles faintly.

"I know you're the Goofball and all, but you need to take our brand more seriously," she says as we exit the bathroom. "Your actions don't just affect you, they affect both of us . . ."

This last part of her speech sounds so eerily similar to what I've heard countless times from my own sister.

"What did you do to get in trouble anyway?" Maddy asks.

I was hoping to avoid the specifics. No such luck.

"I bombed a math test," I confess.

Morgan snickers. "Yeah, right."

"I'm serious."

"You *failed*?"

"Okay, I didn't fail," I said. "I got a C."

"A C?" Morgan is shook. "Isn't it the same math we were doing, like, two years ago? I always get A pluses in math without even studying! You should have asked me to help you!"

There's no way I could have asked Morgan for help. First of all, I vowed never to get tutored by my best friend ever again. It only leads to bad feelings on both sides when I fail. Sophie was the most patient tutor she could possibly be. I cannot imagine Morgan successfully bossing me into being any smarter than I already am.

Plus, asking for help would have been admitting that I needed help. And needing help totally goes against the Goofball Goddess illusion that I'm just, like, *whatever* about my grades and barely spend any time studying at all. But I do. Morgan has no idea how much effort I had to put in just to get that C.

At least I don't have to think about math much longer because Morgan has already moved on.

"Omigoddess," she says. "Here she comes with the Ugly Outfit of the Day!"

I *can't stop it?*

I'm *too afraid.*

How can I be afraid of someone I'm best friends with?

Tan khakis and a navy blue polo shirt isn't a great look, but it isn't horrendous either. Sophie suffers from a lack of fashion imagination. Seriously, she's the only girl I know who would petition *for* a mandatory school uniform. But is that a good enough reason for turning her into a meanie meme?

"Fotobomb! Ummm, Ickface? Pleated khakis are so tacky."

Morgan shoots me a look. I know I'm supposed to play my part. But I'm really, really, *really* not up for it today. I say nothing.

There's nothing there.

Totally blank.

"How do you spell 'khaki'?" Maddy asks for me. "Is it like *T-A-C-K-Y*?"

Maddy is just pretending to be a bad speller. She's always eager to fill in for me when I don't deliver the way Morgan wants me to.

Three weeks into the school year and these daily Fotobombings have become a predictable part of Sophie's routine. But according to Harumi and Sofie-with-an-f, she never sees what's actually being said about her. They saw that as a good thing, but I'm not so sure. Imagination can be our own worst enemy. But Sophie's face is expressionless as she presses onward, pulling her rolling backpack down the hall behind her. Mom warned us in elementary school about the permanent spinal damage that could be caused by heavy backpacks, but only Sophie actually took her advice.

"Isn't Fotobombing Sophie bad for our brand?" I ask when Sophie is out of earshot.

"There's no such thing as bad publicity," Morgan says. "Remember?"

"I never said that!"

"You did too!" Morgan insists.

"I did not!"

In fact, I'm pretty sure Maddy said that, not me. Still, I'm unsurprised when she takes Morgan's side. "You did!" Maddy backs her up. "When you pointed out how Gigi is more popular than the rest of Fourth Dimension . . ."

"But that's not what I *meant*." It's so hard to untwist my tongue when the two of them are staring me down like this. "Aren't we supposed to be positive role models?"

"We *are* positive role models!" Morgan purses her lips. "What's gotten into you today?"

"Nothing," I say.

There's nothing there.

Totally blank.

And maybe on any other day the conversation would have ended there. But I want to prove that Harumi and Sofie-with-an-f are wrong about me. If not to them, then at least to myself.

"I just don't see the point," I say quietly but firmly, "in bullying Sophie every day."

"We are *not* bullying her," Morgan insists. "We're *helping* her. I feel bad for Ickface, don't you? It's like she's actually allergic to cuteness."

"She has no idea how sad she is," Maddy adds.

"And it's, like, our duty to show her what she's doing wrong," Morgan says. "We're doing her—and the world—a service."

Only Morgan Middleton could claim bullying is an act of charity.

Only Morgan Middleton could almost convince me it was true.

ON GUARD

I DON'T SEE SOPHIE AGAIN UNTIL PE. THREE weeks in the same class, and we haven't said a word to each other. It's not that hard. We get undressed and dressed between different rows of lockers on opposite sides of the changing room. And we've actively avoided being assigned the same teams in soccer and flag football. But I'm having trouble getting over what Morgan said about Fotobombing as a favor.

I can't stop Morgan because Morgan is unstoppable.

But I *can* let Sophie know I don't think what she's doing is okay. And hopefully, maybe, that can be enough.

So I'm lingering outside the door to the gym when our gym teacher, Coach Stout, claps twice in my face.

"No time for dawdling, Plaza!" she says. "Line up!"

"But I'm just . . ."

I look back to see if Sophie is on her way out. Coach Stout blows her whistle.

"Line up! We've got a special visit from the university athletic department!"

A half dozen young women and men stand behind her in strappy white jumpsuits that kind of look like straitjackets.

"Today we're going to learn about fencing!"

Bleh. Lauren has told me about these special sports clinics. They were always a highlight for her. As a jock, she loved any opportunity to learn from college athletes. It didn't matter what sport they excelled in: basketball, track, tennis. They worked hard enough to get the kind of scholarship she hoped for—and eventually achieved. But I could not be less interested in learning how to fence. And as I watch Sophie line up next to Harumi and Sofie-with-an-f on the opposite side of the basketball court, I know I'll have to wait until class is over to relieve my guilty conscience.

So the class starts out with us pretending to fence with invisible swords, because I guess it would be too dangerous to equip a roomful of twelve-year-olds with legit weaponry. The university fencers lunge and dip and thrust their real swords, and we lunge and dip and thrust our imaginary swords, and it feels a little childish but isn't very hard because it's kind of like I'm dancing and this is the choreography.

Then we all line up and get a chance to use a real sword called a foil on an electric target. Lights flash, and we're supposed to hit them with the foil before they go off, but no one seems to be doing a very good job at it. They're either too fast and inaccurate or accurate but too slow. And the whole time I'm on line, I'm watching Sophie on her own separate line and I'm thinking about how we went to a midnight release party when the seventh Dragonologist Chronicles book came out. The store hired actors dressed as slayers to reenact the epic sword fight at the end of book six, and I'm wondering if Sophie is remembering that too.

"Plaza! You're up!"

So when it's my turn, I'm not expecting to do much better than anyone else.

Except that I do.

Flash! Ding! Flash! Ding! Flash! Ding!

I hit the lit-up target every. Single. Time.

It's not hard. I'm not even thinking about it. I just do it. And when I finish my turn, Coach Stout asks me if I'd be interested in parrying with a real person. She has not asked anyone else in the class this question, not even the sportiest boys.

"Um, maybe?" I say. "What's parrying?"

And she explains that "parrying" means I'll do, like, a little sword fight for three minutes with a girl named Dede who is a sophomore on the university team. She's got short, spiky red hair, but it's not like Morgan's, which is like an orange hot red; it's more like a purple cool red that doesn't exist in nature.

"Is it safe?" I ask.

"The tip is dull," Dede explains, pressing her finger against the edge. "And bends on impact."

Okay. So I decide to trust Dede that this won't end up like

the book six battle to the death. (SPOILER!!! Sorry!) Dede puts this heavy astronaut helmet on my head that has like, a metal screen I can still see through but protects my face. And she puts me in this Velcro vest that's a less-complicated version of the straitjacket the university fencers are wearing. Then Dede and I square off with an "en garde," and we trade, um, jabs? The clock stops every time Dede's foil touches my vest.

DING!

DING!

DING!

That's one, two, three points for Dede.

And the foils clang clang clang as I try to defend myself from getting poked again with her sword. I know my opponent is going easy on me, but I surprise myself—and the whole class—when I'm able to fake left, go right, and strike her in the ribs.

DING!!!

SCORE!!! ONE POINT FOR ELLA!!!

The gym class erupts in cheers, and I'm totally shocked that I got even a single point in three minutes! When the clock winds down, Dede takes off her helmet and shakes my hand in a show of good sportswoman-like conduct. She and Coach Stout are smiling at me in a way no sporty person has ever smiled at me ever.

"You've got talent!" shouts Coach Stout.

"Yeah, whatever," I say. "She let me score on her."

"Maybe," Dede admits.

"You're quick, graceful, and precise," says Coach Stout.

"Really?"

"Are you kidding me? You riposte with ease!"

I have no idea what that means, but Coach is definitely complimenting me, and now I can't stop smiling too.

"You swear you've never had a lesson?" asks Dede.

"No!" I say. "Unless you count reading all the battle scenes in the Dragonologist Chronicles?"

I wasn't totally kidding, but Coach and Dede laugh really hard at this.

"You're a novice, Ella, but you might have a gift," Coach says.

"You're a natural," adds Dede. "Have you ever thought about taking fencing lessons?"

I shake my head. Of course I haven't thought about taking fencing lessons. I'd never given a single thought to the sport of fencing until thirty minutes ago.

"I teach an Intro to Fencing clinic at the YMCA," Dede adds. "It's just a month-long tryout to see if you like the sport before making a bigger investment. You don't have to buy any of the equipment or the uniform or anything . . ."

I shrug again. But my lack of enthusiasm doesn't dampen their spirits, because both Coach Stout and Dede are still smiling at me as the final bell rings.

Unfortunately, by the time I make it to the changing room, Sophie is already long gone for the day. It's better that way because I never really figured out what to say.

I'm sorry I've got a new best friend who loves being mean to you and I don't even try to stop her.

I'm sorry I've got a new best friend who loves being mean to you.

I'm sorry I've got a new best friend.

I'm sorry.

Morgan and Maddy are waiting for me at the locker room exit.

"Omigoddess, Ella! Your hair!"

I hadn't given a single thought to my hair.

"Oh," I say, patting down the pouffiness. "Gym."

"We know," Morgan says, shooting a look at Maddy.

"You know what?"

Morgan frowns.

"Come on, Ella," Morgan says. "Stop being so modest. You've got a *gift*. You're a *natural*."

I'm baffled for a few seconds. How does Morgan know this? She answers my unasked question by showing me her phone. The university fencing team posted a video and tagged my profile. There I am, sword in hand, looking . . . What did Coach Stout say?

Quick.

Graceful.

And precise.

Morgan is smiling. And for about a split second, I think she's happy for me too.

"Well, it's too bad fencing is for losers and you've got way more important Morgan & Ella business taking up your time." Morgan tugs a springy strand that's fallen out of my ponytail. "And your look is a disaster, Ella! *Disaster!*"

She holds up her phone. I'm expecting to see myself on Fotobomb with a snarky hashtag, like #PhysEdFail. Instead, I see my own unedited reflection. And Morgan is right. My hair is frizzy, and my mascara is raccoon-y, and my skin is greasy.

Disaster.

I guess Morgan is right about the other stuff too.

Fencing is for losers.

Morgan & Ella is way more important.

The biggest deal breaker goes unmentioned:

Fencing lessons are totally unaffordable.

"I'm probably not even that good at it anyway," I say to Morgan.

"Probably not," Morgan agrees.

"I was just the least bad in my class."

"Whew!" Morgan exhales loudly. "Can you imagine willingly subjecting yourself to such uncuteness for a loser activity like fencing?"

Morgan and Maddy shiver at the thought of me even considering that idea for a minute.

Or three.

I take another look at my disastrous reflection in Morgan's phone. Dede's cropped hairstyle makes a lot of sense.

"Can you fix me?"

Morgan smiles and pats me on the head.

"Of course I can, Ella," she says. "That's what I'm here for."

As we head back into the changing room, I think about how much more of a disaster I would be without her.

PRICE TO PAY

IT'S THE DEAFENING KIND OF QUIET IN THE APART-ment, when the hum of the refrigerator roars inside my eardrums like a stadium of booing haters.

I let out a startled yelp when the landline rings at precisely three thirty p.m.

"Lala!"

"Lolo!" I'm grateful for the noise and the excuse to stop pretending I'm doing my math homework. "How did you know I was home?"

Lauren crunches into the phone. Her midafternoon snack time ritual is still going strong.

"Mom told me to check up on you."

And just like that, I'm reminded how my irresponsibility is Lauren's inconvenience.

"What's the big deal? Mom leaves me alone all the time at night!"

"I guess she wanted to make sure you're actually grounded," she says.

"Well, here I am. Home. Grounded. And bored."

Lauren keeps chomping. It's something healthy, for sure, like the driest kind of energy bar without chocolate or even dried fruit to sweeten it up.

"Shouldn't you be doing your math?"

Bleh. Conversations with Lauren are exactly like those cardboardy energy bars.

"Please don't make me talk about math," I say.

"Tell me something else, then." Lauren swallows hard. "I've got five minutes before soccer practice. Go."

Lauren could not care less about Morgan & Ella business. So on any other day, I'd be stumped. But she's probably the only person on the planet who might be genuinely interested in hearing about what happened in PE.

"Well," I say, "our gym class got a visit from the university fencing team . . ."

"Oooooh! Those were always my favorite days!"

It always feels good when I get that kind of enthusiastic reaction out of Lauren. So I go on to tell her about getting a perfect score on the electronic target and being the only one picked to parry with an opponent and Coach Stout telling me I have natural talent . . .

"Cha-ching!" Lauren chants. "Cha-ching!"

Why did I think my record-breaking, award-winning superjock sister would be proud of my pathetic athletic achievement?

"Look, I get it, okay? Fencing isn't a real sport like soccer, but you don't have to make fun of me . . ."

"I'm not! I'm being serious! Fencing is a fantastic sport! There are way too many talented soccer players out there, so it's a lot harder to stand out and get noticed by athletic departments. But not a lot of kids fence, so colleges will come after you if you're the least bit talented."

My sister is an expert on the college recruitment process.

"Are you serious?"

"One hundred percent! The numbers are on your side!" Lauren exclaims. "This is exciting news, Lala! I hope you'll pursue this. It's a lot more sensible than all that silly social media stuff."

Silly

Social

Media

Stuff

As Morgan fixed my hair and reapplied my makeup, Maddy showed me our latest stats. Our newest cover—"The Fullest Truth" by Kaytee K.—racked up a stunning twenty thousand loves in two days. When I first suggested the song, Morgan didn't want to do it because she's more of a Ribot than a Kayter. She only agreed after Maddy convinced her that the OMGs *really* respond to songs with inspirational lyrics.

Stop concealing
Revealing is healing
Give me the fullest truth . . .

I guess we were right! Because our popularity is growing way beyond Paisley and the little girls at the pool! I mean, twenty thousand loves is more than the population of our whole town. Despite my issues with Morgan lately—or, really, *her* issues with *me*—those numbers don't sound very silly to me at all. With this kind of momentum, I'd be a dummy to put anything ahead of Morgan & Ella right now.

I don't expect Lauren to understand, so I sum it up in a way I know she will.

"Fencing gear is really expensive, and we can't afford to pay for the classes anyway," I say. "All that *silly social media stuff* doesn't cost me a thing."

Silence on Lauren's end. Long enough to think we've gotten disconnected.

"Oh, Lala," she says finally, "there's always a price to pay."

NO REFUNDS, NO RETURNS, NO EXCHANGES

WHEN MOM COMES HOME, I GET AN EXACT AMOUNT on one of those price tags.

"So when were you going to tell me?" she asks. "I had to hear it from Lauren?"

It's only been a few hours, but the conversation with my sister already feels like it happened a millionbilliontrillion years ago. In the in-between time, I've been teaching myself songs from all the Disney Princess movies because Morgan decided that would be a way more adorable throwback video than the Spice Girls, who are *too* retro for OMGs to care about.

"Hear *what* from Lauren?"

"That you're taking fencing lessons?"

"No, I'm not," I say.

"Yes you are," she says. "Because she signed you up herself."

"She did *what?*"

Mom shows me the forwarded email from Lauren with confirmation of the registration for Intro to Fencing at the YMCA. It *must* be legit because Lauren only uses email for serious business.

"Since when are you interested in fencing?"

Mom looks baffled, and I can't say I blame her because so am I.

"I tried it in gym class today," I say. "And I told Lauren all about it when she called to check up on me and, well, she got all hyped up about it and started talking recruitment odds and college scholarships and . . ."

Mom chuckles softly to herself. "Classic Lolo."

She's right. It's just so classic Lauren to get RAH-RAH-RAH about something I'm not totally sure I'm even into. Especially when I know for certain it's something Morgan is not into at all.

"Well," Mom says, "you better get at least half as hyped as your sister, because she already paid for it."

I shouldn't be surprised. But I still am.

"SHE DID *WHAT*?"

"She said she had to pay in full," she says, "because the first class is on Saturday."

"Saturday? What time on Saturday?"

"Says here four o'clock."

I can't believe my good luck. I double—then triple—check the time because my good luck is so impossible to believe.

"Four o'clock," I confirm.

Morgan will already be at the equestrian center at four o'clock. She rearranged her calendar to accommodate weekend filming for all the socials, but I guess horses aren't as flexible as humans schedule-wise. With Morgan busy at the stables, I just might be able to get away with these lessons without her knowing.

"You better be there on time," Mom says, "since Lauren can't get her money back."

There, at the bottom of the e-receipt, I see the proof. Fifty dollars. Paid in full. No refunds, no returns, no exchanges. My sister spent her own hard-earned cash—money she earned by mowing lawns and tutoring brats and coaching tiny soccer tots, money she's supposed to invest in herself—on me. She didn't wait for me to ask for it because she knew I never, ever would. And I honestly don't know how—if ever—I can repay her.

Be good, I can hear my sister saying. *Just be good.*

I'll try, I say back.

PART THREE

SO . . . THIS IS ME

HEY, OMGS! WHAT REALLY *GOES ON BEHIND THE* scenes of Morgan & Ella HQ? Here's what you'll never see in our Day in the Life videos.

So . . . as you can tell from all the pink-and-purple animal prints, this is me in Morgan's bedroom. Morgan is scowling because my nails are a disaster. She says I really need to go back and get another Riley Quick manicure because my nails are all torn up from practicing for hours on throwback songs we'll never perform because she changed her mind. I guess that's what happens when you partner up with such a visionary genius. Don't bother telling me if you want, if you really, really want to see that Spice Girls medley I worked on instead of studying for my math test because Morgan is totally over it.

So . . . this is me backing up Morgan on the Disney Princess medley she decided we should do instead. I was kind of surprised by the choice because I made the same suggestion a few months ago and Morgan said that it was too babyish for our brand. But today she's saying that nostalgia is superfun and doesn't she look so regal in that tiara? The Middleton family is modern royalty, for sure! Some of you have asked why Morgan always gets to sing lead even though she sometimes struggles to hit the highest notes. Because she's the Girlboss Goddess, that's why! Thanks to all of you who have said the sweetest things about my harmonies. But I'm supposed to remind you—and myself—that my harmonies wouldn't sound so pretty without Morgan's melodies!

So . . . this is me in my second, third, and fourth outfits of the morning until Morgan finally approves my sparkly hoodie and leggings. We're taking *Morgan & Ella* outside for some location shots all around town, so it's superimportant we perfect the look Morgan is calling Hashtag Weekend Chill.

So . . . this is me with Morgan in Frootie Smoothie in Mercer Square. This isn't spon con, but I wish it were! I'm kind of wiped from trying on all those clothes, and I'm craving a Go Go Greens for its energy-boosting benefits, but it looks like barf so Morgan orders us all the Dragonberry because the pink is so much prettier, don't you think? Do you ever get a food or drink you don't like just because it will look better on Fotobomb than the thing you really want? I can't be the only one, right? Comment below!

So . . . this is me leaving the shop arm in arm with Morgan, sipping our pretty pink Frootie Smoothies.

So . . . this is me going back inside the shop with Morgan to redo our exit because I was squinting into the sun.

So . . . this is me going back inside the shop with Morgan for a third time to re-redo our exit because I wasn't smiling in between sips of my Frootie Smoothie.

So . . . this is me leaving the shop arm in arm with Morgan again, this time smiling and sipping with sunnies on, finally nailing the whole effortless Hashtag Weekend Chill vibe. And I'm strutting down the sidewalk without a care in the world, looking exactly like the most popular girl in seventh grade well on her way to global multiplatform domination, when I lock eyes with the last person I want to see.

So . . . this is me counting down the seconds until four o'clock.

NEW BFF

MORGAN SEES SOPHIE AT THE SAME TIME I DO.

And she also sees that Sophie isn't alone.

"Ummm . . . Lookie who has a new BFF!"

With nowhere to hide on the sidewalk, Sophie is sort of half shielding herself behind this girl we've never seen before. This girl we've never seen before is dressed a lot like Morgan, Maddy, and me, in a rhinestone smiley face hoodie and black leggings. Only Sophie stands alone in her khakis and polo shirt.

The girl we've never seen before bounces up to us, and I'm honestly grateful for the distraction. I'm terrible at keeping secrets—especially from Morgan. All morning I've been afraid of blurting out my plans for the rest of the afternoon: *I KNOW FENCING IS FOR LOSERS, BUT I'M TRYING IT ANYWAAAAAYYYY . . .*

"I'm Kaytee Ray!" chirps the girl we've never seen before. "I spell it *K-A-Y-T-E-E* just like Kaytee K.! I loved your cover of 'The Fullest Truth'!"

Kaytee is smiling not just with her whole face but, like, her whole *body*. She's buzzing with positive energy. With her suntanned skin, swingy ponytail, and springy physique, Kaytee's aesthetic would be something like #SportyChic.

"I've seen all your videos!"

I watch Morgan drop her smirk just long enough to make her most humble face, because Morgan Middleton is the humblest.

"I love you!"

We reply together as we always do.

"And we love you!"

Kaytee shifts her attention in a most unusual way.

"And you must be Maddy, right?"

Maddy blinks in disbelief. She can't believe Kaytee actually knows *her* name. OMGs never pay attention to Maddy.

"I moved next door to Sophie this summer," Kaytee says. "I'm so happy to finally meet you all!"

Sophie is absolutely not happy.

"I love your sunglasses!" Kaytee says to Morgan. "Where'd you get them?"

Morgan yawns. "Oh, these?"

Morgan tried twenty pairs before settling on these oversized white plastic frames.

"And those boots are so cute," she says to me. "I love the stacked heel."

Morgan wore them once, then passed them on to me. She said her ankles were too delicate but mine were thick enough to pull off the look.

"I know, right?" I say.

"And your hoodie is just the cutest," she says to Maddy.

Maddy blushes, totally not used to the attention. Morgan lowers her sunglasses to get a better look at Kaytee. "So you must be in House Two," she says.

Kaytee's face gets all scrunchy.

"House Two? I'm in the house we moved into. Next door. To Sophie."

Morgan keeps her sunglasses lowered, like she's literally looking down on her. She's seconds away from The Eyeroll, I can tell. I've developed a sixth sense for it.

"She means House Two at Mercer?" Maddy explains.

"I don't go to Mercer Middle," Kaytee grumbles. "I go to Ivy Academy."

"Ivy Academy. Well, that explains why I've never seen you before," Morgan says. "The girls there are totally stuck-up."

Kaytee is the opposite of offended by Morgan's comment. She's totally on board with it.

"Yes!"

"And they don't have any boys or any decent clubs or anything."

"Yes!"

"I would *die* if I had to wear that uniform."

"YESSSSSSSSS!"

Kaytee's face is flooded with relief, like finally, *finally* someone gets it.

And that someone isn't Sophie.

Without warning, Morgan clutches Maddy's arm as if she's about to faint.

"Omigoddess! It's *him*."

I don't have time to ask before Maddy answers.

"The Mystery Hottie!" she squeaks.

Kaytee and Sophie turn to see the source of all the commotion: two boys in soccer jerseys exiting All-American Sports.

"Ack." Kaytee gags. "That's my twin brother! And his friend!"

"The Mystery Hottie is your twin brother?" Morgan asks.

"We've been wondering about him ever since he showed up around town last month," Maddy says. "Morgan's totally stalking him."

"I am not!" Morgan snaps. "You're the one with zero chill, not me!"

"He goes to private school too," Kaytee explains. "Wilson Academy."

"He should totally transfer to Mercer!" Maddy says, because it has been established that Maddy has zero chill. "You'll make the cutest couple! I'm shipping you already!"

"What's his name anyway?" Morgan twirls a curl around her finger like the question bores her.

"Alex," Kaytee answers.

"Alex! What should your ship name be?" Maddy muses. "Morgan. Alex. Morgan. Alex. MorLex?"

"Sounds like a laxative," Kaytee jokes. "That's perfect!"

Morgan doesn't crack a smile. Maddy bites her lip. I snort just loud enough that I hope to attract Sophie's attention. If she looks up and catches my eye, maybe . . .

Maybe you'll what? asks The Best Friend in My Head. *Apologize?*

"Come onnnnn," Morgan says, linking Kaytee's arm in hers. "Let's say hi to your brother."

"The other boy is pretty cute too," Maddy says.

The boys are now shoving each other. One's hair is the darkest blond or lightest brown—however you want to call it—just like Kaytee's.

"Hey, Lexi!" Katyee calls out. "You've got a fan club!"

"Lexi!" Morgan and Maddy squeal. *"That's so cute!"*

"Lexi?" asks the boy who isn't Lexi.

"I told you not to call me that!" the boy who is Lexi shouts back.

"He told you not to call him that!"

Morgan and Maddy are falling all over themselves. I guess it's sometimes okay to show zero chill? But only when Morgan thinks it's okay?

"I'm so sorry *Alexander Michael Ray*," Kaytee says with sarcastic emphasis. "I'll never use the family nickname in public again."

"Alexander . . . Morgan . . ." Morgan is deep in thought. "XanGan?"

Alex/Lexi/Alexander Michael Ray grunts a hello. His friend

bounces the soccer ball on his head. He's showing off because that's what boys do in front of girls like Morgan.

I mean, girls like *us*.

Morgan is giving me a funny look. Not ha-ha funny, but curious funny, like I'm the one acting like a zero-chill weirdo and not her. Still another two hours and thirty-five minutes until four o'clock, so I guess I need to participate in this conversation? I make my own awkward attempt at a ship name.

"MorDer?" I suggest.

The friend stops bouncing the ball.

"'Morder' means 'to bite,' in Spanish," he says. "Do you bite?"

Kaytee gags. Maddy giggles. Morgan reaches through the neck of her sweatshirt to adjust the shoulder straps on her bra. I'm still figuring out how to react when Kaytee's twin pulls his friend by the arm and drags him away.

"Let's go, Diego."

"Byyyyyyeeee, Alex!" Morgan and Maddy singsong. "Byyyyyyeeee, Diego!"

I give a little wave but only because I don't want to be rude.

"You're the Mystery Hottie's sister!" gushes Maddy. "You're so lucky!"

I can't hold back my *ewwwww*.

"You realize it would be, like, totally gross for Kaytee to have a crush on her own brother, right?"

"I didn't mean it that way!" Maddy's face turns pinker than her Frootie Smoothie.

"Well, if you and your brother ever decide to transfer to Mercer, be sure to ask for House One," Morgan says. "That's the Cool House."

And then all three of us point our index fingers in the air and make a little whooping sound to pledge our allegiance to the Cool House. I swear I do it without even thinking.

"Well," Kaytee says, looking back at Sophie. "House Two is . . ."

Morgan has no time for talk about the Uncool House.

"Oopsie! Gotta go! Sooo nice meeting you, Kaytee! Tell your brother we said heyyyyy." Then, whispered just quietly enough for Kaytee to miss it, "Bye, Ickface."

As I follow Morgan's lead, I wonder if anyone else noticed what I did:

Sophie didn't say a word the whole time.

FIRST CLASS

ALL DAY I'VE SILENTLY COUNTED DOWN TO MY FIRST fencing lesson. Keeping this information to myself has been both exciting—*I have a secret!*—and excruciating—*I'm keeping it from Morgan!* I was sure she'd see right through me and demand to know what I was withholding from her. And she might have, too, if she hadn't spent the rest of the afternoon obsessively analyzing Alex Ray's socials right up to leaving for the equestrian center.

"Mark my words," Morgan says as she hops into the SUV with Izzy. "The Mystery Hottie will be mine."

Poor Alex/Lexi/Alexander Michael Ray really has no idea what he's in for. But that isn't my problem. I have to bike my butt off if I want to get to the YMCA on time.

"See ya Monday, Maddy!" I say, unlocking my bike.

"Oh," she says, shoulders slumping. "I thought maybe you and I could hang out together . . ."

Maddy and I *never* hang out without Morgan, so I'm caught a little off guard by this request. My excuse is definitely lacking in creativity.

"Sorry! I've got *something* to do," I say quickly. "Maybe another time . . ."

And then I push off and pedal away before Maddy has time to press me for more details.

So now it's finally 3:59 p.m. I've somehow succeeded in showing up for my first fencing lesson without Morgan finding out about it. And one thing is immediately clear:

I don't belong here.

First of all, I haven't stepped foot in the YMCA since Sophie's parents rented out the open play space for her Dragonologist Chronicles–themed eighth birthday party. She invited the whole third grade class, and nearly everyone came. Morgan was one of the few who didn't even RSVP, and I remember Sophie's parents being surprised that a fancy family like the Middletons had such poor manners. The party was no worse—and probably better off—without her. Even kids who weren't so into the books had a blast navigating FlutterFyre's Labyrinth and getting sorted into clans by the Cauldron of Serpentyne. It ended with all of us sprawled on mats on the floor to watch the first movie on a huge screen dropped from the ceiling. And as I cozied up to my best friend, passing a bowl of popcorn back and forth, I remember thinking there would never be a birthday party as fun as Sophie's eighth.

I wasn't wrong.

Second of all, even though this is supposed to be a beginner's class, I'm the youngest person here by, like, five years at least, and, like, five decades at most. Only one out of seven students—a silver-haired senior lady—is wearing the proper white fencing jacket even though it wasn't required. The rest of us—a chubby, red-cheeked high schooler who won't take his eyes off his phone, an extremely tall man who looks like he'd be more at home on the basketball court, and three ponytailed moms who keep congratulating each other for taking "me time"—are wearing normal workout clothes.

At precisely four p.m., our instructor enters the mirrored room. I recognize her right away as Dede, the university fencer I went up against in gym class. Even though it was only a few days ago, I'm still surprised when she acknowledges me.

"Ella Plaza! I'm happy to see you as a last-minute addition to the class roster!"

"My sister signed me up," I say shyly. "After I told her about our, um . . ."

"Bout," Dede says with a smile. "That's what we call a friendly match between fencers."

"What do you call an *unfriendly* match?" I ask.

And that makes Dede and the rest of the class laugh even though I hadn't meant it as a joke.

Dede starts the class by teaching us the basic rules of the sport and explaining how to care for and use the equipment. Her lesson involves a lot of French words and phrases. Some—like "en garde" which translates to "on guard"—are supereasy to remember. "Piste" is the strip on the floor where fencers face off. "Allez" means "go," which is what a referee says to begin a bout. "Corps-a-corps" means there's too much illegal body contact between two fencers.

"We're starting with a foil," Dede explains as she distributes one to everyone in the class. "It's the lightest weapon, with a rectangular blade and dull tip that bends on impact . . ."

Then Dede goes on to explain how competing in foil requires the most discipline because you can only score if you touch the tip of the blade in the area between your opponent's shoulders and waist, and blah blah blah . . . Most of this was already covered in my gym class. Just having that one lesson has put me at an advantage. Despite being the youngest, I seem to have more experience than the rest of the class. It's not often I actually know more than anyone else in the room, and I'm antsy to get jousting. I must not be doing a very good job at hiding my boredom—I've yawned at least twice—because Dede points her weapon at me.

"Come on, Ella," Dede says. "Let's show the class what a beginner's bout looks like."

We stand on opposite sides of the piste.

"Fencing is civilized combat," Dede explains. "Every bout starts with a salute. A gesture of respect."

She swoops her sword through the air in my direction, then does the same toward the rest of class. I imitate her gesture.

"En garde! Allez!"

We both advance, and the swordplay begins. I must have a lot of pent-up energy, because all I want to do is jab and thrust, but Dede stops me every few seconds to explain to the rest of the class what's happening.

"You can only score when you've got the right of way," she says.

"A touch on the arm is outside the target zone and doesn't count," she says.

The interruptions are annoying from a competitive perspective but also informative, so I can't complain because that's what I'm here to do, right? To learn how to get even better at something I might naturally be sort of good at?

The last twenty minutes are spent setting up bouts between classmates. Dede pairs off with Gilda, the senior lady in the fencing jacket. Bob the basketball player partners up with D.J., the high school boy. The two blonde moms—Julie and Jennifer—pick each other. That leaves the brown-haired mom and me. I can tell from personal experience that Heather is annoyed to be the odd one out.

"Well," she says to me, "I bet this class will look great on your college applications."

And I'm glad I'm already wearing my helmet so she can't see the gaggy expression on my face.

I'm twelve! I want to yell at her. *Slow your roll, lady.*

No surprise, it's a very disappointing matchup. Heather actually stops three times because she's afraid she'll break a nail. And when she isn't focusing on her manicure, she's enviously watching Julie and Jennifer giggle their way through their own lazy bout. I wish I could've fought against Dede the whole time, but I can't even imagine how much solo instruction must cost.

We're putting our borrowed equipment away when Dede approaches me.

"You said your sister signed you up?" she asks. "Lauren Plaza, the soccer player?"

I'm not surprised that Dede knows my sister. I get this a lot. My sister has zero Fotobomb followers but is sort of famous in athletic circles. She was All-State two years in a row, and when she accepted her full college scholarship, it was all over the sports blogs.

"Yeah," I say. "That's my sister."

"Well," Dede says with a smile, "looks like there are two star athletes in the Plaza family."

And then she tousles my already messy hair and says she looks forward to seeing me next week. I'm not even gone, and I'm practically counting down the minutes until I'm back again.

FUNDAY

SUNDAYS ARE FOR CLEANING THE APARTMENT.
It used to be the only day of the week I was grateful not to live
in a mansion as massive as Morgan's, until I realized no one
with a mansion as massive as Morgan's actually cleans it themselves. My main responsibilities have always been decluttering
(aka *putting everything back in its place*) and dusting. Since
Lauren left for school, Mom and I split up her duties, so now I
have to vacuum too. Mom has taken on mopping.

When Lauren, Mom, and I work together, we can get the
whole place done in about an hour. I'm terrible with numbers,
but since Mom and I split her jobs in half, *mathematically* it
should only take Mom and I, like, thirty minutes more to clean
the whole apartment without Lauren, right? But it hasn't worked
out that way. Mom and I are learning that like everything else,
Lauren was an overachiever cleaner.

Mom bends down to inspect a scuff mark on the kitchen tile.

"Your sister got this floor cleaner in five minutes than I can in twenty!"

I turn the vacuum back on to avoid hearing another word about Lauren's efficiency. My first-day-of-school peace-sign tee has been shedding bling all over the apartment since its last run through the washing machine. No matter how aggressively I push the vacuum over the carpet, the same stubborn sequins refuse to get unstuck.

This would make the worst Day in the Life video ever.

Hey, OMGs! So . . . this is me in my Dragonologist Chronicles T-shirt and flannel pajama bottoms because it's laundry day and I'm all out of cuteness! Vacuuming sucks. Ha ha! Get it? Stick around, and you'll get to see me use a toilet brush! Jealous much?

Mom taps me on the shoulder. I can't hear her over the roar of the vacuum. But I don't have to hear her to understand.

Just pick them up, she pantomimes. *If you keep running the vacuum over the same spot we will have nothing to show for our efforts except a hole in the carpet.*

Mom is very expressive even without words.

I shut off the vacuum and get down on my hands and knees to pinch the sequins from the carpet fibers. An oldies pop song from Mom's youth is blasting from the speakers.

"*Roam if you want to,*" Mom sings along to the stereo. "*Roam around the world.*"

It's a bouncy pop song, sung by two women in lively unison

that splits into harmony. Mom is smiling as she sings it, which is weird to me because this song makes me think of my Secret Map and how maybe our father might have taken those lyrics a little too much to heart.

I turn the vacuum back on so I don't have to hear the rest of the song.

My mother is a terrible singer. Her voice lands in this tuneless space between alto and soprano, and if I didn't already dislike this song, her version isn't turning it into a fave. On Sundays, Mom always plays music from her youth at a very specific volume: loud enough to sort of sound like a dance party but not so loud that the neighbors complain. When I was younger, I could be tricked into thinking that vogueing to Madonna with my very own feather duster was a fun way to spend a Sunday. When I was younger, a lot of things made me happy because I didn't know any better.

The vacuum powers down all on its own. I jab the on/off switch a few times before I notice Mom is swinging the unplugged cord in her hand.

"You're not getting this apartment any cleaner," she says. "At this rate you'll never be done."

"Why rush? It's not like I'm allowed to go anywhere or do anything fun when I'm done."

Mom leans on her mop. She's got bags under her eyes, and her hair is corkscrewing out of control.

"That's not fair," she says. "I let you spend a whole Saturday with Morgan Middleton."

"I wasn't with her the *whole* day," I say. "I had my fencing lesson too . . ."

Mom has had very little to say about my fencing lessons. I think she's a little mad at Lauren for signing me up without her permission.

"If Morgan wants to come over here today to help you with your chores," Mom continues, "she's welcome anytime."

Ha! Morgan Middleton has never run a vacuum or touched a feather duster in her life. Unlike me, she doesn't need to wait for global multiplatform domination to hire a staff to do all her dirty work.

"Morgan has way more important things to do on a Sunday," I reply. "She's *optimizing* all our *social media content* for *maximum engagement* . . ."

Mom twists her lips and turns away to rinse the mop in the kitchen sink.

Mom can barely figure out Facebook—and that's, like, *designed* for old people. She doesn't even know what Fotobomb is. So I get why she doesn't understand why Morgan & Ella's growing popularity on the socials is such a big deal, even when I use fancy words like "optimizing." But why can't she see how Morgan & Ella's success will make life better for her too? When we start making major money, I'll buy Mom a massive mansion and a whole staff to clean it.

I don't say any of this though.

I surprise her—and myself—by telling her something I hadn't planned on mentioning at all.

"We ran into Sophie yesterday."

Mom shuts off the faucet and turns to me. She instantly looks less exhausted than she has all morning.

"Really? How is she? You know she's always welcome over here *any*time. Even after school. Maybe she could help you out with math . . ."

I can hear the eagerness in her voice. She wants Sophie back in my life so badly, and Mom needs to know that friendship isn't an option anymore. I give her the only reason that won't make her lips all twisty.

"Sophie has a new best friend, Mom," I say. "A really cool girl named Kaytee whose family moved in to the house next door."

"Ella," Mom says, tucking a loose curl behind her ear, "just because she's got a new friend doesn't mean she doesn't have room in her life for an old friend."

And before I can stop her, she's singing that cheesy Girl Scouts song:

Make new friends, but keep the o-old.

One is silver, and the other's gold.

Mom's singing voice is the second worst in the world. She's only outdone by Lauren who—of course, in her weirdly competitive way—has to be the very best at being the very worst singer. I've always wanted to know if I inherited my musical talent from our father. I've never had the courage to ask.

"I hated Girl Scouts," I confess. "I only did it because Sophie did it."

Because we did everything together, says The Best Friend in My Head.

"Girl Scouts taught you about goal setting," Mom says. "I wish you'd apply those lessons to your schoolwork."

Mom has no idea what she's talking about.

Sophie lived for earning badges for her sash. *Our sashes.* I earned all the same honors as she did—from Junior Activist to Zoologist—but didn't get excited about them in the same way Sophie did. To get me motivated, she'd even let me pick out the badges that looked most interesting to me—Jeweler, Scribe, or Musician, for example—but I'd always lose interest less than halfway through the checklist. I have to think our troop leaders knew Sophie was doing most of my work, too, even though that was totally against the Girl Scout honor code. The only part I genuinely liked about Girl Scouts was standing up in front of the rest of the troop and harmonizing with Sophie on the "Make New Friends" song. When I was younger, an audience of a dozen Scouts was enough to make me happy. Now I'm not sure how many Fotobomb followers it will take.

A sunbeam shoots through the window and highlights a missed sequin at my feet. I pick it up and show it to my mom.

"Can I be done now?" I ask.

Mom sighs instead of saying yes.

How many Sundays did Sophie come over to help clean the apartment? She was the one who pointed out how the feather duster just kind of moved dirt around and that it would be much more efficient and still environmentally friendly to trap grime with a reusable microfiber cloth. With her obsessive eye for detail, Sophie didn't make us any quicker, but definitely better.

"Sophie isn't fast," Mom would joke. "She's *fastidious*."

Lauren is both.

I'm neither.

But it doesn't matter. If our brand makes us as rich as Morgan promises it will, we'll never spend another Sunday pushing vacuums and mops.

PERFECTION INSPECTION

MORGAN AND MADDY BURST THROUGH THE DOOR to the girls' bathroom on Monday buzzing with news.

"Have you seen the Fotobomb numbers?" asks Maddy.

"Of course she hasn't," Morgan says. "She never sees anything."

Maddy slaps a drumroll against her thighs to hype up the big reveal.

"Morgan got *five thousand one hundred and three* new fans this week!"

Maddy is doing all the boasting because Morgan is the humblest. I react in a very high-key way, but that's okay because that's part of my Goofball charm.

"Wowza! We're really blowing up!"

"Ummm . . . Not *we*." She ding-dongs her head. *"Me."*

"Not you," Maddy emphasizes. *"Morgan."*

Maddy shows me her phone while Morgan casually checks her mascara in the mirrors above the sink. Morgan's numbers are exploding all over Fotobomb. Less than a week ago, she was two hundred followers behind me, and now she's pulled ahead by five thousand-ish? And with 15,109 followers, she's got more alone than Morgan & Ella do together.

"What can I say?" Morgan says with a cute little shrug. "The fans love me."

I'm still trying to process all this information—*5,103 new fans in a week???*—when Morgan rattles a plastic shopping bag at me.

"Special delivery!"

Morgan doesn't bring new outfits for me every day. But it happens often enough that she's totally stopped telling me white lies like *Oh, I thought this would look cute on me but it looks way cuter on you* so I'll feel less awkward about it. It's clear she's buying these items specifically for me because I can't be trusted to shop for myself.

As I undress in the stall, Morgan and Maddy gossip about that girl and her brother we met on Saturday.

"Kaytee already follows Morgan & Ella on all the socials," Maddy says, "but it's totally tragic that the Mystery Hottie does not."

"His name is Alex," Morgan reminds us. "And he won't be a mystery to me anymore if I have anything to say about it."

Morgan says it like someone who always has something to say about everything. This poor boy has absolutely no clue what he's in for.

"Ella! Come out for inspection! The bell's gonna ring soon!"

I stuff my comfy jeans and tee into the shopping bag and step out of the stall in a floral jumpsuit that feels too tight in some places and too loose in others and not like me at all. But I shove those thoughts aside like I did with my first outfit of the day. I put on a smile and do a little spin and avoid looking at the price tag because this store's clearance racks are still way out of my budget.

"Perfection!"

If my best friend wants to share a tiny fraction of her wealth, isn't it an insult to reject her generosity?

Oh, Lala, there's always a price to pay . . .

I don't correct my frowny face fast enough.

"Awww . . ." coos Morgan.

"Awww . . ." coos Maddy.

Morgan puts on a supersympathetic face and pats me on the shoulder.

Maddy steps aside and lets her have this moment all for herself.

"Don't feel bad. You've still got a bunch of fans who are into your aesthetic."

First, this jumpsuit doesn't feel like my aesthetic. And second, I don't feel bad at all. I'm sort of relieved to have proof that Morgan is more popular than I am.

Even if the proof is . . .

Well . . .

I don't want to sound jealous.

Or petty.

Or like I know more about the socials than Morgan and Maddy do. I mean, I'm straight out of the nineties with my phonelessness.

But.

Five thousand one hundred and three new fans in less than a week is . . .

Suspicious?

"So," I say, casually applying a fresh coat of lip gloss, "I guess the, um, algorithm worked itself out?"

"Ummm . . ." Morgan puckers for the mirror. "Obviously!"

"It only makes sense for the Girlboss to have more followers than the Goofball," Maddy says reassuringly. "Balance is restored."

"Right," I say. "But . . ."

But I thought we were supposed to be equals, I don't say. *And this imbalance just makes us look bad as a brand . . . ?*

"Selfies!" orders Morgan.

The light is perfection and our poses are perfection and our Fotobomb posts are perfection.

clickclickclickclickclick

How can the rest of my day . . .

Spanish verbs I can't conjugate

cells I can't find under the microscope

math problems I can't solve

. . . possibly live up to this perfection?

POSITIVES AND NEGATIVES

TRYING TO ACT NORMAL IN FRONT OF MORGAN AND Maddy is exhausting. I'm not the most focused student even on my best day. So I hear very little of what Miss Lee has to say about similes and metaphors. I don't process much of Mrs. Munson's PowerPoint about Pangaea. My brain is too pre-occupied with a question that won't appear on any upcoming test.

What if Morgan dumps me for someone with a better aesthetic?

By the time we separate for foreign languages, Morgan & Ella is just about the last thing I want to think or talk about. Unfortunately, our number one OMG has her own burning questions.

"What's up with your socials lately?" Paisley asks as she slides into the seat next to me in Spanish class.

"I know, right?" I reply. "The numbers are pretty bonkers."

"Well, yeah," she says. "But I'm talking about all Morgan's videos. Where are you?"

"What do you mean?"

Confession: I haven't voluntarily watched any of our videos since I lost my phone. I won't look away if Morgan or Maddy shoves a phone in my face, but I haven't gone out of my way to see myself on-screen. To be honest, I've always enjoyed making the videos more than I ever did watching them. I see too many mistakes—wrong notes, wonky tempo—too late to correct. If I ever gave more thought to the foreverness of my fails, I'd never step in front of a camera again.

"She's posted a bunch of videos that are just about her," she says.

"What are you talking about?" I ask. "I was with her all day on Saturday shooting content."

Paisley shakes her head soberly.

"Well, you'd never know it," she says. "Like, the only video you were in was the Disney Princess medley, and that's only because it wouldn't make any sense without you on the ukulele or the harmonies. And even then the camera was tight on her face, and you were, like, just barely seen over her shoulder . . ."

"So what's she doing in all these other videos?"

"She's, you know, being a Girlboss," Paisley explains. "Morgan at soccer practice, Morgan on her horse, Morgan in dance class, Morgan . . ."

Well, that would sort of explain the sudden surge in

followers . . . right? Did Maddy put her up to this? To make sure I. DID. NOT. GET. MORE. POPULAR. THAN. MORGAN?

Paisley is just getting started, but Senora Greenbaum commands us to "abren sus libros," and we have to wait another forty minutes to finish the conversation because we don't have the vocabulary to say it in Spanish.

"So you really had no idea she edited you out?" Paisley asks the moment class ends.

"No!"

"The OMGs are not going to stand by and just let this happen!" Paisley starts texting frantically. "We are Team Ella all the way!"

"No! No! No!" I grab her phone out of her hands. "I'm sure that Morgan has an overall strategy. She would never do anything to damage our brand. You should tell the OMGs Hashtag Goalz Girlz is going strong . . ."

Paisley, who is probably Morgan & Ella's most devoted fan, isn't buying it.

She chatters all the way to math class, which even on the best of days is the worst.

"You know this is *exactly* how Fourth Dimension broke up," she says. "Gigi blew up on Fotobomb faster than the rest of the girls in the group. Pippa got jelly because she was supposed to be the lead singer, and she talked Joy and Niecy into trashing Gigi all over the socials and sharing those terrible pics of her . . ."

Paisley is practically tearing out her double buns just thinking about it.

"That's not going to happen," I assure her.

"It would be so tragic for Morgan & Ella to break up when you're so close to global multiplatform domination."

Then we have to stop talking about it again because we've got a test on negative integers that I had totally planned to study for on Saturday until Morgan rearranged her busy schedule to record content instead. I'm all shaky and sweaty, and I can't tell if I'm more upset about Morgan or this test.

I try to remember the rules.

$-25 + 25 = 0$

The sum of any number and its opposite is zero.

$25 + 25 = 50$

Adding two positives is always positive.

$-25 + -25 = -50$

Adding two negatives is always negative.

$25 - -25 = 50$

A minus sign followed by a negative sign . . . turns it into a positive sign? Can that be right? That doesn't sound right. How can two minuses turn into a plus? That seems to go against all logic. And now I'm starting to panic because I have no idea how I'm going to confront Morgan and Maddy about cutting me out of all this weekend's videos. Or Sophie about . . . what, exactly?

It's too many negatives and not enough positives, and every answer I come up with is zero.

NEXT LEVEL

SO WE'RE SITTING DOWN TO LUNCH, AND I'M STILL
doing a very bad job at being normal. Fortunately, Morgan is
laser focused on her phone instead of me.

"Omigoddess!" Morgan squeals. "It's happening!"

"What's happening?" Maddy asks.

Morgan's thumbs are blurry, she's texting so fast.

"Kaytee is transferring to Mercer Middle School!"

It takes me a moment to remember who she's even talking
about.

"The girl with Sophie?" I ask.

"The Mystery Hottie's twin sister?" Maddy asks.

Alex. Lexi. Alexander Michael Ray. The Mystery Hottie.

"Yes!" Morgan literally pats herself on the back. "She's
transferring to Mercer, and it's all because of me!"

In between nibbles of baby carrots, she tells us how Kaytee

hated the stuck-up girls at Ivy Academy but couldn't convince her parents that public school would be any better until she told them all about meeting us and how sweet and totally not snotty we were even though we totally could've been because we're on the verge of global multiplatform domination . . .

I am stunned.

I had no idea that Morgan and Kaytee had been in any contact with each other since we ran into her on the sidewalk. This is clearly news to Maddy, too, because she hasn't even opened her own Ziploc bag of baby carrots.

"What House?" Maddy asks.

"The Cool House, of course." Morgan twirls her finger and whoops. "She wouldn't have known to ask for House One if it hadn't been for me. None of this would be happening if it weren't for me. If Kaytee hadn't run into me on the sidewalk, she would still be stuck at Ivy Academy. She'd still be settling for Ickface just because she happened to move in next door. *I* made Kaytee see how much better her life could be!"

Morgan's phone buzzes, and she looks at the screen and laughs. She doesn't bother sharing the joke.

"Anyway, Kaytee obviously has no idea what she's gotten herself into with Ickface," Morgan says. "We need to tell her what's what before her reputation is permanently trashed."

I hate to admit this because we only met verrrrry briefly, but it *is* strange that someone like Kaytee would be best friends with Sophie. They make an odd pair. Kaytee is superfun,

Sophie is serious. Kaytee is pop cultural, Sophie is pop clueless. Kaytee is faboosh, Sophie is . . . well . . . forgettable.

Morgan and Kaytee . . . ?

Now that's a friendship that makes sense.

"Alex and I are *so* destined to be a couple!" Morgan points a celery stick at me. "Which means you and his best friend, Diego, are destined to be a couple!"

Me? And Diego?

"How do you know?" I ask.

"Because—duh!—that's just how these things work!"

Diego is funny and all, but I don't think I'm really all that interested in having him or anyone else as a boyfriend. There are some uke cuties I kind of crush on when I'm watching their tutorials, but I'm not ready for a relationship IRL. I watched Lauren suffer high school heartbreaks, and I want no part of it.

Not to mention what happened between Mom and our father.

"It's too bad Kaytee's not into music," Morgan says. "But she says she was the best girl on her soccer team in Virginia, so I was like, 'Omigoddess! You have to try out for Squad Goals!'"

"Squad Goals?" Maddy asks.

"Ummm . . . that's what we call ourselves," Morgan replies. "We're the best travel soccer team in the state. Maybe even the East Coast. If she's as good as she says she is, she should totally have no trouble making the team!"

Morgan looks at her phone and laughs at another private joke too hilarious to share with me. My only consolation? Maddy isn't in on it either.

SECOND CLASS

I'VE NEVER BEEN A TEACHER'S FAVORITE BEFORE.
But I'm the best in my fencing class by, like, a lot. The Moms
are too giggly. Gilda is too hesitant. Bob is too large a target.
D.J. is too asthmatic. And though there's not much competition
for the top spot, it still feels pretty great to be a positive example
others can learn from.

"Footwork isn't just about the feet," Dede says, adjusting
the angle of my shoulders. "It's about getting the whole body in
balance from the ground up."

Dede always chooses me to demo new maneuvers, so it's
almost like I'm getting one-on-one instruction. And I'm taking
in these lessons, like, on a *physical* level, because when I'm in the
middle of a bout, it's not at all *mental*. I'm not really thinking
about anything but getting a hit on my target. It's automatic in
a way that I can only compare to when I used to pick up and

165

play the ukulele for fun, without worrying about whether the song would go over well with the OMGs or if I'd have to master the whole thing in a different key because Morgan couldn't hit the high notes.

Again, the hour goes by too quickly.

I leave the fitness center happy about the lesson but also sad because I've only got two more lessons left. I guess my brain is too caught up in this battle to pay attention to where I'm going because I crash right into someone exiting the room next door.

"Owwww!"

"Omigoddess! Sorry!"

And I'm so startled by the collision that it takes me a few seconds to recognize who this boy is.

"Kaytee's brother, right?" He's rubbing his shoulder. "Alex?"

"Yeah," he says. "I'm Alex."

We're walking in step with each other now toward the exit.

"I'm Ella," I say. "You probably don't remember me . . ."

"I remember you, from downtown," Alex says. "You were the only girl who didn't act like a fool."

The *only* girl who didn't act like a fool? This doesn't seem possible. He must be mistaken. I have to fix this error—and fast.

"No, you're confusing me with Morgan," I say. "She's the cool one. I'm the goofy one."

"Nope," Alex says simply.

He pushes the door and holds it open for me to go through before he does. Who knew the Mystery Hottie had such impeccable manners? The blast of chilly autumn air feels refreshing after such a sweaty workout.

"Well," I say, pointing to the bike rack, "I'm pedaling home."

"I'm running," he says. "Good cardio for soccer."

"Oh," I say. "Okay. Right! Were you practicing with your soccer team today?"

The question doesn't make any sense. The room next to ours is a mirrored dance studio. Alex isn't wearing a soccer uniform and is the only boy exiting the fitness center among a group of graceful girls wearing leotards with tightly wound buns in their hair . . .

Like ballerinas.

"Something like that," Alex says in a rush. He doesn't offer any more of an explanation. But his cheeks are blazing pink, and for some reason I don't think it's from exercise or the wind.

"See ya around!" Alex sprints away on the sidewalk. Obviously, he doesn't want me knowing any more than I already do. And that's fair, because I don't want him knowing any more about me either.

FITNESS TEST

WELL OVER A MONTH INTO MIDDLE SCHOOL, AND I'm still wondering how to go about talking to Sophie in gym class.

This is the type of dilemma Mom totally does not understand, because as much as she loves sharing life lessons, I don't think she remembers what it's really like to be a twelve-year-old girl. She'd tell me to walk right up to Sophie in the locker room and just start talking to her. As if it's *just that easy*. She doesn't get how weird that would be. I can't just walk up to Sophie and start talking to her like oh, no big, I haven't been avoiding her for ages. It's not as drastic as sitting with the same two girls at lunch every day and then suddenly deciding to sit at a totally different lunch table in a totally different section of the cafeteria with a totally different group of girls, but it's pretty darn close.

Leave it to Coach Stout to provide an awkward solution to my awkward situation.

"It's that time of year again!" She pumps her fists. "Physical fitness testing!"

The whole class gags in agony, but nothing can dampen Coach Stout's enthusiasm for this annual assessment of our athleticism—or lack thereof. Recent victories in fencing aside, I am not expecting to rock this test. She blows a whistle to put an end to our moaning and groaning.

"Pair up!"

I don't have any friends in this class. Sophie's friends—Harumi and Sofie-with-an-f—choose each other. The *sorry-not-sorry* shrug they give Sophie instantly reminds me of Julie and Jennifer from fencing class. As much as I'd like to believe that as adults we'll all outgrow this kind of pettiness, the blonde moms are living proof that—sadly—some girls never do.

"You two." Coach points at me, then Sophie. The leftovers. "Pair up!"

We barely look at each other as we trudge over to the gym mats on the floor. We're starting with sit-ups. Coach instructs us to take turns. One holds feet and counts, the other crunches. Then switch.

Neither of us is eager to get started.

"Do you want to go?" I ask. "Or should I?"

These are the first one-on-one words I've spoken to Sophie in over a year.

"I don't want to do this at all."

I wince. She's talking about all this—being with me—not just lying down on a gym mat that reeks equally of socks and bleach to crank out as many sit-ups as she can in sixty seconds.

"Okay," I say, lowering myself to the mat. "I'll go."

We haven't so much as brushed shoulders since sixth grade. It's just so weird that we're, like, forced to invade each other's personal space like this. She's visibly skeeved to grab hold of my sneakers.

"This is very unsanitary," she says, crinkling her nose.

Coach Stout blows the start whistle before I can argue. Or agree.

Sophie gives me credit for thirty-five crunches in a minute. I would've given myself thirty-six, but I was less than halfway up on the last one and Sophie is a stickler for rules and regulations.

We don't say anything when we swap spots on the mat.

I take hold of her ankles and notice for the first time that she isn't wearing plain white tennis sneakers. She's wearing a sportier brand, the kind I often see on Brianna and Hailey and the other interchangeable girls on Morgan's soccer team. Are the sneakers Kaytee's influence?

Sophie's jaw is set in the way it gets when she's determined to succeed at something. At the sound of the whistle, she curls upward and loudly blows out a puff of air.

"WHOOSH!"

She sucks in air as she leans back.

"SHOOHW!"

Curl up, blow out.

"WHOOSH!"

Lean back, suck in.

"SHOOHW!"

She does this over and over again, fast at first, but slowing down as the seconds tick away.

"WHOOSH!"

"SHOOHW!"

Sophie probably watched a documentary about this exercise breathing technique, like, ten years ago and never forgot it, because she's got the kind of brain that remembers everything it ever needs to ace tests—even a stupid sit-up exam in remedial gym class.

With five seconds left, she's on crunch thirty-four . . . thirty-five . . .

"Come on, Sophie!" I cheer. "You can do it!"

The whistle blows as she falls back with a final *"SHOOOOOOOOOOOOHW!"*

"Thirty-six! One more than me!"

She totally earned it by sitting all the way up on the last one. She's red faced and panting . . . and totally pleased with herself.

"I didn't think I could do so many!"

"Oh, I knew you could do it," I say. "You *were* the underwater karaoke champ."

Sophie cracks the tiniest smile at the memory of one of the silliest games we used to play at the Mercer Community Pool.

The rules were simple: We'd plunge below the water's surface, and one of us would sing a pop song while the other tried to guess what it was. Sophie came up choking the first few times we played, but she got really good at it—even better than me.

"Next up! Flexibility testing!" shouts Coach Stout.

This one is supereasy. All we have to do is sit and stretch our arms as far as we can go.

"Oh, I like this one," I say. "With my monkey arms, I've got an advantage."

A silent puff of air escapes Sophie's lips. It's not a laugh exactly, but close enough that I feel victorious, like I completed 360 sit ups in 60 seconds.

"Lauren only said you had monkey arms to torture you," Sophie says. "I'll never understand why siblings bully one another like that. You should see the battles Kaytee and Alex get into!"

She sits and extends her legs next to mine. This conversation is flowing so easily. I close my eyes and imagine we're eleven years old again, side by side on beach towels in the shade, swapping damp copies of the Dragonologist Chronicles . . .

I wonder if Kaytee likes the same books.

I wonder if Kaytee plays underwater karaoke.

I wonder if Kaytee is good at school.

I wonder if Kaytee will like me.

"You must be so happy about the news," I say.

Sophie tenses.

"What news?"

Sophie pushes her hair behind her ears, as if it will help her hear me better.

"The news," I say, "about Kaytee."

Her face is a blank. Either Sophie has watched a documentary on how to make the perfect poker face or she honestly has no idea what I'm talking about.

"Kaytee is leaving Ivy Academy and coming to Mercer."

Sophie's jaw drops.

My stomach drops.

"How do you know this?" she asks in a small voice.

I really don't want to be the one to tell Sophie her new best friend shared her big news with Morgan, not her. Hearing it from me—her ex–best friend—will only make this sucky situation even worse.

"How do you know this?" she repeats, even quieter.

"I guess she's been texting Morgan and . . ."

All the color drains from Sophie's face.

All the hope.

"She's doing it again." A whisper.

Morgan is stealing my best friend, says The Best Friend in My Head. *Again.*

And if Morgan is successful . . . what does that mean for me?

Coach Stout blows the whistle.

"Next up! Chin-ups!"

Sophie barely grips the bar before letting go.

She limps the shuttle run.

Lies down for push-ups.

I can't believe what I'm seeing. This is worse than just giving up. Sophie—the most focused and determined girl I know—is failing on purpose. I hate that Morgan has such power over her.

Over me.

Over all of us.

"Ella!" Coach Stout claps me on the back as I'm heading to the locker room. "Make sure you come see me after class today."

"Okay," I say.

But I already know I won't.

I don't even change my clothes. I grab my backpack, race out of school, and run all the way home.

DING-DONG

BY THE TIME I GET HOME, MY BODY IS ACHING FROM
the inside out and back again. It's not from the run or the
Presidential Physical Fitness test.

The discomfort definitely goes deeper.

I pace around the apartment, telling myself I have nothing
to do with what's going on between Sophie, Kaytee, and
Morgan. But I know it's not true. We're all connected.

If Sophie weren't my ex–best friend . . .

If Morgan weren't my new best friend . . .

If Kaytee weren't Sophie's new best friend . . .

If Morgan . . .

If Kaytee . . .

If . . .

If . . .

If . . .

DING-DONG!

I nearly jump out of my skin at the sound of the doorbell.

DING-DONG!

I creep to the peephole, hoping to see a Girl Scout I can quietly ignore.

"Open up, Ella!"

Morgan rings the bell again. And again. And again.

DING-DONG!

DING-DONG!

DING-DONG!

"I know you're in there!"

I take a deep breath before unlocking and opening the door.

"Oh, hey, Morgan!" I'm all casual. "What's up?"

Morgan pushes her way past me.

"What's up with *you*? Where were you after school today? I *waited* for you. I was just standing there all by myself by the flagpole like a loser, and it was totally embarrassing."

"Alone? Why? Where's Maddy?"

"I told her I was having a mascara emergency." She says this as if it's the most normal thing in the world.

"Your lashes look amazing."

"I know that!" Morgan says testily. "It was just an excuse for you and me to have a moment to ourselves. I have huge news! And you had to ruin it by being all weird and totally ditching me for no reason after school today."

"I'm sorry, Morgan." I look away. "I needed to do, um, something. For my mom . . ."

She looks me up and down.

"Well, it must have been important for you to go out looking like *that*."

"Very." I cross my arms in front of my Mercer Middle gym shirt. "Important."

I think Morgan doesn't believe me, but I also think she doesn't care. Whatever she has to tell me is more important than my excuses.

"So remember how I told you that girl Kaytee is transferring to Mercer?"

How could I forget?

"Well, I haven't even told you the best part about it!"

Morgan strikes a very pleased-with-herself pose. This is called *milking a moment*. It's another classic Riley Quick maneuver that Morgan has practiced and perfected.

"Kaytee's mom works in PR and can take Morgan & Ella to the next level of fame and fortune and followers!"

Morgan pirouettes and takes a bow.

"How?" I ask.

"By getting us meetings with bigwigs in the industry, that's how!"

"She can do that?" I ask. "Like, for *real*?"

"For real!"

Morgan communicates in hyperbole, a language arts term I recently learned that means "extravagant exaggeration." So until this moment, I've taken her most ambitious promises only so seriously. Sure, I entertain myself with dreams of living in luxury and never spending another Sunday scrubbing toilets. It's fun to fantasize about world tours and endorsement deals and photo shoots. Morgan & Ella is an escape from my boring, often disappointing reality. But now Morgan's telling me an actual adult with industry experience is on board with our brand? It's like blasting off on a rocket to superstardom without a seat belt.

Speaking of language arts terms, says The Best Friend in My Head, *that's a great simile.*

I need to slow down.

"What about Maddy?" I ask.

Morgan is circling my apartment. She runs a finger across our glass coffee table, then rubs the nonexistent dust with her thumb.

"What *about* Dunzo?"

Dunzo.

Maddy is Dunzo.

"*Maddy*," I say, ignoring the new nickname, "is doing a pretty great job. Think about all those new followers you got last week."

Morgan rolls her eyes.

"I know you can't help but think small, Ella."

She's not wrong. Morgan has been preparing for greatness all her life, but it's all so new to me. I watch as she presses the wobbly ceramic key dish until it tips over.

"With a team of social media professionals, our number can decaduple!"

Math is not my thing, and I doubt "decaduple" is even a word, but I get what Morgan is saying.

"But don't tell Maddy she's out," Morgan says. "I don't want her to know until it's, like, a done deal."

Based on Maddy's unenthusiastic reaction at lunch today, I'm wondering if maybe she already knows?

"Ella!" Morgan snaps her fingers in front of my face. "Are you even listening to me?"

"Of course," I lie.

"So I can count on your renewed commitment to the brand?"

Morgan is in full Girlboss mode. She's a seventh grade CEO of the universe. There is no messing around here.

"Yes."

Morgan breaks out into her most dazzling smile, the one she usually saves for selfies.

I'm prepared for her to give me a list of songs to learn and looks to perfect before bouncing out the door to her soccer team, her horses, and her dance class. But she's still here, looking closely at a framed photo on the wall. It was taken at Lauren's high school graduation. She's in her cap and gown, and Mom and I are hugging her on both sides. It's not the most flattering picture—I'm squinting and Lauren's smile is too gummy and Mom's curls are flying all over the place—but we're happy. And there aren't many pictures of the three of us. We asked one of Lauren's classmates to quickly snap it for us.

When Morgan abruptly turns, I'm expecting her to warn

me against ever posting an unflattering pic like that on Fotobomb.

"So what can you tell me about your dad?"

I'm taken aback. Like, literally. I stumble backward into the couch cushions, but I try to play it off like I'm just messing around. There's only one friend I've ever talked to about my father. And she wants nothing to do with me.

"Earth to Ella!" Morgan sings. "I asked about your dad."

It's so weird to hear Morgan call my father "dad." I've never called my father "dad." He's never been a dad.

Morgan flops down on the coach next to me.

"My people can't find anything on John Plaza, anywhere."

"Your people?"

"My family does background checks on everyone we associate with," she says. "But we can't find anything about your dad."

Morgan's people can't find anything on my father because they must think Plaza is *his* last name. But it's not. It's Mom's.

That's how *not* a part of our lives this man is.

"Why would you need to know about my father?"

"You know I hate bringing this all up, but my parents are very important people," she says. "We just have to be very careful about who we associate with . . ."

"Well, I don't *associate* with my father," I croak. "He's never been around long enough."

"But where is he *now*?" she asks.

Croatia? It's been ages since I updated my Secret Map. He could be all the way on the *other* other side of the world by now.

I shrug and hug a pillow and pray Morgan takes a hint and stops asking questions I can't answer.

"I see this is very hard for you." She throws an arm around my shoulder. "As a Middleton, I'll never go through what you have. Your struggle is, like, *really* real."

I'm about to thank her for understanding when Morgan's phone buzzes. She springs from the couch.

"Gotta go!"

She's almost late for soccer practice. She tells me what songs to learn and reminds me what look to show up in tomorrow. #TGIFierceFriday. Then she's out the door less than five minutes after she arrived, already on to the next big thing.

Morgan Middleton is determined to take me along for the wild ride, whether I'm ready or not.

CLOSE ENOUGH

I SHOULD REHEARSE SONGS ON MY UKULELE.

I should practice fencing footwork.

I should get my #TGIFierceFriday look ready for tomorrow.

I should do my math homework.

I should study for my Spanish test.

I should fix my manicure.

I should confront Morgan.

I should warn Maddy.

I should check up on Sophie.

But I can't do any of those things.

My conversation with Morgan has left me feeling too confused.

And too curious.

Mom won't be home for a few hours. And there's only one

other person who might be able to add to the short list of what I know about our father.

Our father met Mom on a cruise ship en route to the Bahamas.

Our father was a steward; Mom was a housekeeper.

Our father was twenty and without a diploma; Mom was eighteen, a new high school graduate earning money for community college.

Our father got Mom pregnant somewhere in the Caribbean Sea.

Our father stayed on the cruise ship; Mom moved in with Grandma and put college on hold.

Our father promised to marry her.

Our father didn't marry her.

Our father visited Mom and Lauren whenever he docked in nearby ports.

Our father got Mom pregnant again.

Our father didn't promise to marry her this time.

Our father knew Mom wouldn't believe him.

Our father sails around the globe on crews for chartered yachts.

Our father hasn't seen us in nine years.

Our father contacted Lauren last month.

This isn't enough. I need more. Not for Morgan, but for myself. I pick up the phone at the first ring.

"Lolo!"

"Oh no." My sister blows a long, low whistle. "What's wrong, Lala?"

One advantage to being sisters with a know-it-all: Lolo sees right through me, even from five hundred miles away. She doesn't even bother asking me about the fencing lessons she's paying for or anything else. What a relief that I don't even have to try to pretend like everything's fine.

"What's the deal with our father?" I blurt.

Lolo reacts in a most unexpected way. She laughs.

"Oh, Lala, I expected you to ask for advice about a typical middle school problem."

"What's a typical middle school problem?"

"Like, you got your period in the middle of gym class and bled through your shorts but you're still kind of freaked out by tampons . . ."

I would've preferred stained shorts over what happened with Sophie or Morgan's interrogation.

"That's very specific," I say.

"Guess why," Lauren says with a groan. "Anyway, I'm sort of not prepared to have a deep discussion about our nonexistent father. I'd much rather hear about your fencing class . . ."

"It doesn't have to get deep," I say, cutting her off. "I'm just . . ."

Confused. And curious.

"Did something happen?" she asks. "Why now?"

"I just . . ."

No way I can tell her about Morgan's background check. If Morgan's people have investigated our father, then they must know Lauren's AP results, goals scored, and financial aid package. I'm not even famous yet, and Lauren's privacy is already being violated. I honestly never gave much thought to how fame might negatively affect *her*.

I never gave much thought to how fame might negatively affect *me*.

Lauren exhales.

"So you never found your phone."

"No."

It's funny how little I think about not having a phone. Even funnier to think that my Fotobomb numbers—though not as bonkers as Morgan's—are bigger now than they were when I was hashtagging all the time. Not having my phone hasn't been a *disaster* at all. I honestly don't miss it. Not one bit.

"So you couldn't see or reply to his texts."

This news totally takes me by surprise.

"He . . . texted me?"

"That's what he says."

"Does Mom know?"

"Of course! I checked in with her first before replying to him. I didn't want to do anything to upset her."

Lauren would *never* do anything to make Mom's life harder.

"So you've actually texted him back?" This news takes me even more by surprise. "I thought you wanted nothing to do with him."

"I wanted nothing to do with him when he wanted nothing to do with us," she says. "But he's been making an effort lately. I think it's something to do with the fact that he's scheduled for a charter that starts in the Virgin Islands and ends . . ."

"In New Jersey?"

"New York," she answers. "But maybe that's close enough for a visit."

A visit? From our father? For the first time in nine years? I can already predict Morgan's response to this news.

Ha! Usually deadbeat dads reappear after their kids get rich and famous!

"Lala! What are you thinking?"

St. Thomas, St. John, and St. Croix make up the US Virgin Islands. Tortola, Virgin Gorda, Anegada, and Jost Van Dyke make up the British Virgin Islands. All these islands are already crossed off my Secret Map. Our father has come this close before but has never made it all the way to see us.

"I'm thinking," I reply, "about how you and Mom knew all this and didn't tell me."

"He's made promises before," Lauren says. "We didn't want you to get your hopes up."

"My hopes aren't up," I say. "When it comes to our father, I don't have any hopes."

You know that's not true, says The Best Friend in My Head. *I've seen the map.*

Lauren gulps a lungful of air.

"I guess that makes one of us."

I've never heard my sister sound so . . .

vulnerable.

And all at once, I understand why this conversation hasn't happened before.

Lauren wasn't protecting me.

She was protecting herself.

"I gotta go, Lala," she says. "But if you want to talk about this later, I'm here."

"Here" meaning "there."

Meaning "not here."

Is that an oxymoron?

In a weird way, I have Morgan to thank for this new information about our father. So why isn't she automatically the first person I want to confide in?

Why do I still talk to The Best Friend in My Head?

PART

FOUR

IS THIS ME?

OH . . . HEY, OMGS. DID YOU MISS ME? I MEAN, US?

There's so much happening at Morgan & Ella HQ lately. We made some major changes to our team and, well . . . it got a little hectic and we didn't post on the regular. Don't panic though. Morgan & Ella is coming back Girlbossier and Goofballier than ever . . .

At least that's what Morgan tells me!

So . . . this is me and Morgan walking down the hall with our faboosh new friend Kaytee on the way to language arts! If you look carefully, you can see Maddy following right behind us. Our new formation isn't personal; it's practical. There's just not enough room in the halls for us to walk four across. "It's not personal; it's practical" is how Morgan explained to Maddy that her research and promotional services aren't needed anymore. Morgan's learned a ton from watching her politician father and put it that way because she *thought it would make Maddy feel less angry about being let go, but I don't think it worked, and . . . whoopsie! I'm blabbing way too much! But what do you expect from a Goofball like me?*

Just look at them. Aren't Morgan and Kaytee just the very definition of sporty chic in their matching Squad Goals jerseys? Morgan—as all you OMGs know from her new series of Girlboss Lessons solo videos—is as talented on the soccer field as she is on a mic. And I guess Kaytee is too, except for the on-mic part. Kaytee is superadorable, but don't expect to see her singing along with Morgan and me, because she has zero musical abilities . . .

At least that's what Morgan tells me!

I don't know much about soccer, but I guess Morgan is something called a striker, which sounds exactly like a position she would play. I don't know Kaytee well enough to say if she's accurately cast as a defender. All I know is that their positions do offensive and defensive things, so Morgan won't compete against Kaytee for playing time, which is crucial for maintaining the balance in their new friendship. Because as totally fun as it is having another seventh grader on the team, having another seventh grader on the team means Morgan misses out on the special status of being the only seventh grader on the team. Not that Morgan is, like, worried about the New Girl outshining her or anything because duh, that would never, ever, ever happen . . .

Morgan didn't have to tell me that. It's something I already know very well.

Kaytee moved to New Jersey from Virginia over the summer, but she just started at Mercer Middle because her parents made her try the snooty school we've promised to never, ever talk about that rhymes with Schmivy Schmacademy. She's got a twin brother, Alex, who caught Someone's attention this summer. That Someone is determined to make him transfer to Mercer too. Kaytee says Alex loves his school and there's no way Morgan—Whoopsie! There goes my blabby mouth again!—I mean, Someone will convince him to leave, but that's only because Kaytee doesn't know Someone as well as I do and . . .

BONK!

A GRAPE BOUNCES OFF MY FOREHEAD AND PLOPS onto my pizza.

Morgan chucks another grape at me, but this time I duck and it lands on the floor behind me with a squish.

"Have you heard a word of what I'm saying?"

I have not. I've been too preoccupied by the made-up video in my mind.

Morgan pokes Kaytee in the ribs with a plastic spoon. For the past week, it's been the three of us at a table that's really meant for two. It definitely can't fit four, which is why Maddy has been eating her lunch in the computer lab lately. She says it's because she's working on an extra-credit project for Digital Citizenship, but I know better. If Sophie had lunch this period, would Kaytee have insisted we make room for her? Or would she have chosen to sit at Sophie's table with Harumi and Sofie-with-an-f instead of with Morgan and me . . . ?

Another grape bonks me in the nose.

"Ella's mind wanders," Morgan says.

"Oh," Kaytee replies with a smile. "Mine does too. Sophie is always laughing at me for going off on random tangents."

I doubt Sophie has ever laughed *at* Kaytee. Only *with* her.

"So you and Sophie still hang out?" I ask.

Morgan yawns in a very dramatic, wide-awake kind of way.

"Well," Kaytee says, her shoulder slumping slightly, "not as much as over the summer. I thought we'd see more of each other once I transferred to Mercer. But with the two-House system here, we barely cross paths! We still walk to school together every day, but now that I'm busy with the travel soccer team after school . . ."

Morgan finishes her sentence for her.

"You're friends with *the* most popular girls," she says. "All thanks to me."

Kaytee sits up a little straighter.

"Maybe not *all* thanks to you," she replies.

Morgan freezes, her yogurt spoon in midair.

"Don't get me wrong," Kaytee continues. "I'm happy you told me about the team tryouts, but I got on the squad because I've got skills." She takes a long gulp of her blue sports drink. "I'd like to think the other girls like me for who I am and not just because of who I know."

Morgan lets out a little gasp. The New Girl obviously doesn't know not to talk to a Middleton like that. I'm literally on the edge of my seat, waiting for her retaliatory roast.

It doesn't come.

Morgan quickly rearranges her face.

"Of course you earned your spot! And of course they like you for you! Who *wouldn't* like you?"

Morgan isn't wrong. Kaytee is incredibly likeable. But would Morgan be putting in so much effort if she didn't have a Mystery Hottie brother? Or a mom with PR connections?

For the next few minutes, Morgan complains about the other girls on the soccer team.

"Brianna is such a ball hog. And Hailey shows no leadership skills."

I stab at my lunch with a fork. As a connoisseur of baked dough topped in sauce and cheese, school square-style is probably the least appetizing of all shapes and forms of pizza. But it's particularly cardboardy and flavorless today. I never thought lunch would rival math or gym as my least favorite period of the day. I've pretty much murdered my meal when Kaytee unexpectedly turns to me.

"So, Ella," she says, "can I make a request?"

I'm so surprised to be seen as a decision maker that I automatically look to Morgan for approval. She gives a tiny nod.

"Um, sure."

"Can you arrange another Kaytee K. song on the ukulele? She's my absolute fave!"

I wait for a second nod from Morgan.

"Sure," I say. "Which one?"

"Surprise me!" Kaytee exclaims. "I'm Morgan & Ella's hugest fan, and I'm Kaytee K.'s hugest fan, so it will be just the fabooshest cover ever!"

If Paisley were here, she'd argue with Kaytee on the first point and easily give up the second. I think they would quickly come to agree on the third.

To prove her fandom, Kaytee breaks into what technically could be considered a song, but it's so off-beat and off-key that I'm not sure it actually qualifies.

"sToP conCeaLInG revEALinG is HeaLing GiVe mE tHe fuLlest TruTh . . ."

I haven't heard Morgan laugh this hard since I fell off the bleachers.

"Omigoddess, Kaytee!" Morgan gushes. "You are so hilarious! Our fans would love you! I wish you'd appear on camera!"

"Nope." Kaytee shakes her head. "I'm much more comfortable behind the scenes."

"Speaking of, your mom is still looking into hooking us up a public relations team, right?"

Morgan mentions it so casually, as if she hasn't been dying to ask Kaytee this question all day. Morgan never wants to give the impression that she needs anyone else's help. Even when she so clearly does.

Kaytee bounces up and down in her seat and the whole table-for-two wobbles.

"Totally!" Kaytee answers. "She's been out of the business for a few years but still knows people . . ."

Morgan startles.

"What do you *mean* she's out of the business? You told me she worked for a major PR firm!"

The table shakes, and loose grapes escape to the floor. And after seeing the icy-hot look on Morgan's face, I'm about two seconds from dropping to the ground for safety myself. Kaytee downs the last of her drink and crushes the bottle as if nothing is wrong.

"Well, she did, until she took time off to raise me and my brother . . ."

Morgan cuts her off.

"So your mother is not *currently* a public relations professional?"

"Technically, no," Kaytee says. "But she's looking to get back into it. My mom thinks you two are really talented and really wants to help you . . ."

Morgan has stopped listening. She's now giving her phone the attention Kaytee Ray no longer deserves. I search the New Girl's face for hints of trouble, but she beams as brightly as her radiant last name. She looks and sounds 1,000 percent sincere and not at all concerned about being liked for who *she* knows.

But that's only because she hasn't spent as much time with Morgan as I have.

NEXT TO LAST CLASS

MY THIRD OUT OF FOUR FENCING CLASSES IS already over. It was the best one yet. But it definitely didn't seem like it would go that way when Morgan called me up this morning just to complain about her horseback riding lessons.

"The horses stink, and the helmet messes up my hair, and I'm just so over it!" she griped. "But my parents are forcing me to go, and it's torture and not fair!"

Not fair? For the price of just one session at the equestrian center, I could take fencing lessons for six months! But I obviously couldn't say this to Morgan. I didn't know what to say that wouldn't sound like I was accusing her of being a spoiled brat, so I kept my mouth shut.

"Helllooo? Ella? Are you there? Did we get cut off again?"

I was never so grateful for the landline. I quietly hung up, unplugged the phone from the wall, and spent the next few hours getting *really* worked up. It's a fact that the Middletons will throw away more money on "torturing" their daughter with expensive activities than my mom will earn in a lifetime. Now *that's* unfair.

I was still feeling stabby when four o'clock rolled around. Fortunately, fencing class is probably the most perfect place on earth for this particular emotion. I was prepared to conquer a whole squadron of fire-spitting dragons, so poor Bob didn't stand a chance.

"En garde!" he called jovially.

"En grrrrrrrrrrrrrrrrrrrrrrrrr!" I growled in return.

I defeated D.J., Gilda, and The Moms in similarly epic fashion. I thought I'd feel a bit drained after the second or third victory, but instead of losing energy in each bout, I actually gained it. Only it was a different kind of energy, as if through the swordplay I'd transformed anger and negativity into power and positivity. By the time I finished fencing against Dede herself, I felt downright invincible—which is ironic because it was my only loss of the afternoon.

And now there's only one lesson left.

The Moms, D.J., Bob, and Gilda have just cleared out, but I'm lagging behind. I'm not in any hurry to put this class behind me, so I'm very slowly stowing my borrowed gear.

Dede pokes me in the shoulder with her foil.

"So how do you think these lessons are going?"

They're going . . . going . . . almost gone, I think. *And* that's *not fair.*

I'm feeling the fuzzy burn behind my eyes and at the back of my throat. If I try to talk, I'll cry. So I just shrug instead.

"Let me tell you how they're going," she says. "They're going pretty freaking great."

It means a lot to hear this from Dede. I'm not delusional. I really am as good at fencing as I think I am.

"That's why you're the only one in the class I'm encouraging to go to this."

Dede shows me a neon orange paper with the university and county logos at the top. Sure, I've seen these flyers posted all around the fitness center, but I haven't actually bothered to read beyond the first line of bold, large font:

FENCING FOR ALL.

Not for me, I thought the first time I saw one pinned to the bulletin board. *Not for long*.

"I can't," I croak. "I mean, we can't."

I don't want to say it out loud.

We can't afford any more lessons. One month was already too much.

And even though she isn't even here, I find myself getting mad at Morgan all over again. I'm not jealous of her exactly, but I do envy all the opportunities she takes for granted. Her parents would buy the YMCA and rename it in her honor if she showed even the teensiest smidge of interest in fencing.

I throw down my protective chest pad and flee the room before I have to say any of these humiliating truths aloud. I'm so eager to get away that I don't even notice Alex lingering in the hall.

"Heeyyy . . ." he calls out, but I've already sped past him toward the exit.

"No time!"

"Whoawhoawhoawhoawhoa!" he says, reaching the doors before I do. "What's the rush?"

I make him wait until I'm safe before giving him an answer.

"I needed to get out of there before I could feel any worse," I say.

His eyes get all crinkly in a way Morgan thinks is "the cutest thing ever, ever, ever."

"Are you *really* that bad at fencing?" he asks.

"No," I say. "I'm great at fencing. But my lessons end next week, and I'm upset because I won't be able to keep going . . ."

I don't give any more details, and I really hope Alex doesn't ask for them.

He doesn't.

"I'm sorry," he says finally. "That sucks."

What a relief. Sometimes all I want is someone to, like, validate my bad mood and not try to talk me out of it. Alex is still walking with me toward the bike rack, though, so I guess that means our conversation isn't over yet.

"I'm taking a ballet class," he says.

I pretty much figured this out already. So I'm not surprised by the confession itself, but I absolutely wasn't expecting him to make it to me. It takes a lot of confidence to be the only boy in ballet class. Lucky for him I happen to think that kind of confidence is very, very cool. But I guess he's nervous I'll judge him harshly. He watches my face carefully for a reaction.

"Wow," I say. "That's very, very cool."

"Dance can be helpful cross-training for soccer," Alex explains quickly, defensively, as if he's already prepared himself for pushback. "It improves balance, core strength, and agility."

"I know," I say. "My sister took yoga for the same reason."

"Oh," he says. "You have a sister who plays soccer?"

Alex just moved here from Virginia. He has no idea who my sister is. What an unexpectedly happy turn this conversation has taken.

"Don't tell anyone, okay?" Alex asks. "Diego would roast me so hard if he found out I was spending my Saturday afternoons in dance class."

"Why are you telling me this?"

"I don't know why," he says. "You seem like someone I can trust."

We reach the bike rack, and I start spinning the numbers on my combination lock. I literally cannot afford to have this bike stolen, so I'm usually sort of paranoid about not letting anyone catch a glimpse as I enter the code. But I don't even try to shield the lock from Alex's eyes.

I don't know why, but he seems like someone I can trust.

"I can't tell anyone about my fencing class either."

"Including that Morgan girl, right?"

His lip curls when he says her name. Morgan would not find his disgust very cute at all.

"*Especially* that Morgan girl," I reply.

He flips up his hood and cinches the strings.

"Your secret is safe with me."

"Yours too."

We fist-bump to make it official. And though I should be happy about making an unexpected new friend, I'm already worried about what will happen when Morgan inevitably finds out about it.

FREE TALENT SCHOLARSHIP

NOW THAT WE HAVE A FRIEND IN COMMON, IT FEELS even weirder for Sophie and me to continue ignoring each other in gym class. But it's so easy to ignore someone when the person you're ignoring is equally committed to ignoring you right back. Like, if she's striking out at bat, I'm in the farthest outfield. If I'm missing all my foul shots, she's waiting her turn on the away team bench. If she can't stop the hockey girls from scoring on her goal, I'm doing the same poor job in my goal all the way on the opposite side of the field.

So another class has ended, and I'm picking up the yoga mat I placed as far away from Sophie as possible. Coach Stout calls out to me on the way to the locker room.

"Plaza!" She blasts her whistle at me. "Let's have a talk!"

"Am I in trouble?"

I fell flat on my butt when attempting tree pose.

"No, not at all," she says, smiling broadly.

Coach pats the bench for me to sit down. Then she props up her foot and leans on her knee.

"Dede got in touch with me," she says. "Says you're showing a lot of progress and promise in her class . . ."

Which ends next week, so why does it matter?

"Which is why she was encouraging you to sign up for this . . ."

She flips through the papers on her clipboard and holds up the same orange flyer Dede showed me on Saturday. I'm already shaking my head, but Coach does not have time for my excuses or explanations.

"Plaza! Did you even *read* it?" Coach Stout asks, barely hiding her irritation. "It's an opportunity to get *free* instruction . . ."

Free?

"It's a talent search . . ."

Talent?

"Winners of the beginner's tournament get a full scholarship . . ."

Scholarship?

She goes on to say stuff about how this is "a joint Town & Gown initiative," which means the community leaders and the university are working together on it. I guess they want to make a bunch of expensive sports like fencing more inclusive to athletes of all socioeconomic backgrounds, but really the only details I need are . . .

FREE

TALENT
SCHOLARSHIP.

Coach Stout says more stuff about how it's expected to draw first-time fencers from all over the state, so getting a scholarship isn't guaranteed. But Dede wouldn't have pushed the idea unless she thought I was ready. Just like Lauren wouldn't have spent her own money for me to fail. I'm not used to having so many people believe in me. What if I don't live up to their expectations?

It feels good but scary too.

Even scarier? The prospect of Morgan finding out about it.

"The tournament is Monday after school at the university fitness center," Stout says, handing me the flyer to take with me. "And if you need a ride, I'm happy to work something out with your parents."

"Paren*t*," I say, sharper than I meant to. "My mom."

I haven't asked any more questions about our father lately. And Lauren seems all too happy to not have to answer.

"I apologize," Coach says in a softer voice than normal. "I can make arrangements with your mom."

I catch Sophie exiting the locker room with Harumi and Sofie-with-an-f. If it weren't for her, I wouldn't already know the university campus is exactly 1.2 miles away from my apartment. That's a five-minute drive, ten-minute bike ride, twenty-minute walk.

"No need," I assure Coach Stout. "I'll get there all by myself if I have to."

I fold up the flyer and slip it into my hoodie's kangaroo pocket.

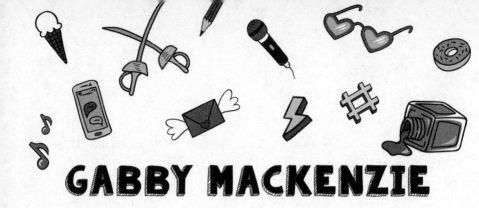

GABBY MACKENZIE

I SWEAR THE CLOUDS WAIT UNTIL I STEP OUTSIDE
to unleash all the rain they've been holding on to all day. It was
sunny when I left for school this morning, so, of course, I'm
totally unprepared for such a drastic change in the forecast.
Sophie, Kaytee, Harumi, and Sofie-with-an-f are impossible to
miss on the sidewalk in front of me, all four girls fully protected
by a ginormous golf umbrella in FlutterFyre stripes of green
and orange. There's no room for me under that umbrella, and
I wouldn't have sought protection underneath it even if
there were.

I brace myself for a soggy trudge home, thinking about
how much I sort of envy Sophie. She doesn't care one bit
about clothes or hair or makeup or boys or any of the things
that girls our age are supposed to care about. She doesn't seem
to worry about being blasted on Fotobomb every day. She

doesn't know the first thing about global multiplatform domination. She isn't embarrassed to walk around school all day
with a ginormous green-and-orange-striped golf umbrella
that doesn't fit in her locker because she checked the weather
forecast and saw there was a 99 percent chance of rain during
her walk home.

Okay, so she's a bit nerdy. But Harumi and Sofie-with-an-f
have accepted her as she is. And now she's got Kaytee on her
side too . . .

"Yoo-hoo! Earth to Ella!"

A hand frantically waves at me from the back window of a
Mercedes SUV.

I've got Morgan.

Without hesitation, I jump into the back seat.

"Thanks for the rescue!"

"Whoop! Practice is canceled! Let's get hot chocolate!"

I open my mouth to remind her that I'm grounded when
she leans back and takes a critical look at me.

"Ummm . . . You look like a drowned rat. No offense." She
taps Izzy on the shoulder. "Quick detour to Morgan & Ella HQ
for damage control. Then hot chocolate!"

"Why can't we just get hot chocolate?" I ask.

"We can't put you on the socials looking like that!"

"Why do we have to put it on the socials?" I ask. "Can't we
be just, like, two ordinary seventh graders getting hot chocolate
on a cold, rainy day?"

Morgan pinches her lips, shakes her head slowly.

"Ella . . ." I know what she's going to say. And I almost say it with her. *"Why do you think so small?"*

"I don't think *small*," I reply. "I think . . ."

I think *what*, exactly? Morgan doesn't give me time to figure it out.

"You miss being best friends with Ickface?" she asks. "Because I can think of at least twenty thousand OMGs who would trade places with you in a millisecond. And you can be as ordinary and as boring as you want to be."

She's got me there. Because here's the fullest truth about being best friends with Morgan Middleton: It isn't always fun. But it's *never, ever* boring.

"So let's get you looking perfect, let's get some hot chocolate, and let's get you home before your mom ever knows you were gone."

I know I should still tell her to tell Izzy to take me straight home. But Morgan is so hard to say no to when she's Girlbossing as hard as she is right now. I plunge my hands into the front pocket of my hoodie and run my fingers over the flyer like it's a protective amulet, which is just about the wrongest thing I can possibly do in front of a noticer like Morgan.

"Are you hiding something in there?"

And before I can stop her, she's sticking her hand inside my pocket and practically arm wrestling with me over possession of the flyer.

"Morgan! Stop it!"

"No, *you* stop it!"

She successfully wins the paper away from me, takes one look, and pops off.

"Ella! We *talked* about this! No fencing!"

I avoid looking at Morgan as she reminds me of all the reasons why fencing is a nonstarter. Instead, I stare at the back of Izzy's head and count gray hairs. One . . . two . . . three . . .

"Off-brand . . ."

Four . . . five . . . six . . .

"For losers . . ."

Seven . . . eight . . . nine . . .

"Terminally uncute . . ."

"Ella!" Morgan snaps her fingers in front of my face. "Does the name Gabby Mackenzie mean anything to you?"

Morgan knows way more people than I do—online and in real life. It's impossible to keep all the names straight.

"Is she one of the eighth graders on your soccer team?"

Judging by the lemon-sucking pucker on Morgan's face, I am incorrect. The rain has eased up. How bad would it be if I asked Izzy to just drop me off right here and let me walk the rest of the way home?

"Gabby Mackenzie was Riley Quick's best friend in middle school," she explains. "They were in a band together called Mack & Quick. She played drums and sang harmonies."

"That's not true."

"It is *too* true," Morgan says. "Look it up on QuickWiki."

It doesn't seem possible that I would miss this important part of Riley Quick's bio. But it seems equally unlikely that Morgan would make this all up on the spot.

"So what happened to Gabby Mackenzie?"

"Nothing," she says. "Absolutely nothing happened to Gabby Mackenzie. Because she wanted to live an ordinary, boring life. So she went to high school instead of going on tour. Mack & Quick broke up, and Riley Quick went solo and got enough fans to sell out arenas all over the world and make her the number one most followed celebrity on Fotobomb. Gabby Mackenzie wanted to live an ordinary, boring life. And that's exactly what she got. No fame. No fortune. No followers."

Morgan says it like this is the saddest, most pathetic fate that could ever befall a twelve-year-old girl. As the gates open wide to let us onto the Middletons' property, I'm realizing just how much Morgan has invested in me.

This is about so much more than just friendship.

And yet.

Global multiplatform domination often feels like so much less.

BEING GOOD

MORGAN COMES THROUGH ON HER PROMISE. SHE
gives me a rainy-day makeover, buys me hot chocolate, posts
the cutest pics on the socials, and sends me home with Izzy
before my mom can ever suspect I've been gone. Best of all,
Lauren has a game today, so I don't even have to come up with
an excuse for why I've missed her daily phone call.

And yet, I'm not surprised at all when Mom has barely
shaken the rain out of her hair before targeting a question right
at my guilty conscience.

"So, Ella," she says, kicking off her damp Crocs, "do you
have anything to tell me?"

This is such a classic Mom question. "Anything" could
mean literally *anything*.

Do I tell her I was getting hot chocolate with Morgan when
I should have been home doing my math homework?

Do I tell her I still think of Sophie as my best friend even though we don't talk anymore except in my head?

Do I tell her I'm keeping a secret for a boy and he's keeping one for me?

Do I tell her Morgan is looking for dirt on my father?

Do I tell her Lauren is getting her hopes up again?

The questions are big and small and in between, and it's no wonder I don't have any leftover brain space for the preterit tense, organelles, or order of operations.

"No?" I reply uncertainly.

Mom's eyes light up and she playfully tousles my hair.

"Your gym teacher called me about the fencing tournament!"

"She did?"

"She did," Mom replies. "She offered to take you if I'm not free."

"I told her not to do that! Are gym teachers even, like, *allowed* to bother busy moms with phone calls at work?"

Mom laughs. She's wearing her favorite pink scrubs. Though her gloss has worn off and her hair is wet and wild, she's still prettier than any other parent when she relaxes.

"I'm glad she called! This sounds like an incredible opportunity. And you never even mentioned it to me!"

"I just found out about it! I'm probably not even that good!"

"Well, Coach Stout seems to think otherwise. She says you've got real talent."

I can't remember the last time I heard such pride in Mom's voice.

Not for Lauren.

For *me*.

"Actually," I add, "she says I'm quick, graceful, and precise."

Mom places a hand to her chest and inhales deeply, like she really, really wants to take in this big moment.

"Doesn't it feel good," she says, "to be good at something?"

Be good.

Be good.

Be good.

Hot chocolate bubbles in my belly like a kettle of poisonous Wyvernweed.

"Because unlike Lauren, I'm *not good* at school and everything else that's important?"

Three big stomps and I'm in my bedroom, slamming the door behind me.

I'm not even sure how Mom's pride in me turned into a fight about Lauren. I flop onto the bed and bury my head in the duvet. I don't want to hear Mom knocking on my door, and I don't want to give in to her demands for an apology.

But the knock doesn't come.

And neither does the demand.

She leaves me alone in my room to feel even guiltier, which is worse than any lecture.

I should use this time to:

1. Learn all the new songs.
2. Work on my look.
3. Perfect my aesthetic.

But I don't want to do any of those things Morgan wants me to do.

I should use this time to:

1. Do my math homework.
2. Write my language arts essay.
3. Study for my Spanish test.

But I don't want to do any of the things Mom and Lauren want me to do.

For the first time in ages, I'm drawn to the bookshelf.

With so many doubts about my own life, there's something comforting about returning to stories I already know end well. And no book, in my honest opinion, does it better than *The Dragonologist Chronicles: The Epic Conclusion*. When I pull the book by the spine, something clatters to the floor. I assume it's a forgotten eyeshadow palette or an unopened contouring kit. There's just enough space for me to wedge my hand between the wall and the shelf to retrieve . . .

AHHHHHH.

A shot of recognition zips through me.

HAAAAAA.

My phone.

I
finally
finally
finally
find
my
phone.

I immediately press the on button, which is totally pointless because the battery died ages ago. The monogrammed case is missing a rhinestone. My first thought: No way Morgan will tolerate an imperfect *E*. She'll present me with a fully blinged replacement before I've even had a chance to shop for one myself.

So all I have to do is plug in, charge up, and catch up on all the action I've missed since summer. I turn my phone over and over and over in my hands.

Over

and

over.

Three months of missed and mixed messages will only confuse me even more than I already am.

I don't plug it in. I don't charge up.

I put down the phone, pick up my favorite book, and read.

TOMORROW TODAY

SWORD IN ONE HAND, PROTECTIVE AMULET IN THE other, I'm defending the hatchlings from a wicked sorceress with hair as fiery as dragon breath. She wants them all for herself. And she won't rest until . . .

"Ella!"

Mom shakes me fully awake.

"Ella!"

When I sit up, *The Epic Conclusion* slides off my chest and falls onto the floor with a weighty *thunk*.

A dream.

I must have fallen asleep during the Battle for Crystal Caverns. The light is grayish, and I'm so disoriented that I can't tell if it's morning or night. Yesterday or tomorrow.

"Ella," Mom repeats. "The phone is for you."

Mom's wearing yellow scrubs.

It's tomorrow.

Meaning today.

Morning.

"Phone?" I mumble groggily. "But I . . ."

But I decided not to plug in my phone . . .

"The landline," Mom explains, reading the baffled expression on my face.

"The landline?" I knuckle sleep out of my eyes. "Who'd call me on the landline so early in the morning?"

"Morgan Middleton," Mom says in a clipped voice reserved for her name alone.

I bolt from the bedroom and pick up the receiver. Mom decides this conversation isn't worth showing up late for work and heads to the bathroom to finish getting ready.

"Morgan? Why are you calling me so early? I'll see you at school."

Nothing can prepare me for Morgan's highest-key reply.

"Ella! We have a meeting with Ribot Entertainment!"

I swear half of me is still on the battlefield defending those dragon eggs.

"Ella? Did you hear me?" Morgan is legit shouting. "We! Have a meeting! With Ribot Entertainment!"

I'm still dreaming, right? There's no way I'm hearing what I'm hearing.

"Ribot Entertainment?"

"Riley Quick's management team!" Morgan squeals. "They're looking for fresh talent! And Riley Quick is dedicated to supporting female artists! This is the boost from a major influencer we've been waiting for! I told you it would happen for us!"

She did. And yet, I honestly never believed celebrity could happen for someone like me. It's for other girls like Morgan Middleton, who are nervy enough to think bigger than everyone else. Now that I've teamed up with a winner, fame and fortune and followers are possible for me too.

I shout, "OMIGODDESS!"

She shouts, "OMIGODDESS!"

We shout, "OMIGODDESS!"

For the first time in forever, it feels like it did back in the beginning of our friendship, when Morgan approached me at the start of sixth grade and said, very matter-of-factly, "I like your look." Her approval made me feel like the most important girl in this or any universe.

"So we're actually meeting Riley Quick?"

Morgan heaves a sigh.

"Ella, Ella, Ella."

Morgan's most condescending singsongs are always in perfect key.

"We're meeting with Riley Quick's *management team*. That does not mean we are meeting with Riley Quick. Riley Quick, as you should know, is in Tokyo right now, on the Asian leg of her international tour."

"Oh," I say.

"Riley Quick is far too important to meet with girls like us."

"Oh."

"One day *we* will be far too important to meet with girls like us."

"Oh."

"Your naivete is so . . ." If we were in the same room, she'd pat me on the head. "Sweet."

I don't think I'm, like, *exceptionally* naive. Morgan is exceptionally all knowing. There's a big difference. But my excitement cannot be squashed by the weight of Morgan's condescension. Not today.

"I can't believe this is happening!" I gush. "I guess Kaytee really came through for us, huh?"

"Kaytee has *nothing* to do with this," Morgan replies sharply. "Daddy's people set this up for us."

"But . . . what about Kaytee's mom?" I ask. "Isn't she . . . ?"

"That whole family is canceled," says Morgan dismissively. "I should've known they weren't to be trusted when Kaytee couldn't even get her loser brother to reply to any of my texts."

Hearing Morgan refer to Alex that way makes me choke on my own breath. And she's not done yet.

"Those two are, like, the Flaky Twins."

The Flaky Twins. That's a new one.

RIP MorLex.

And what does it mean for Kaytee?

"Besides, Daddy's people are way higher up in the new media industry," she says. "We've got so much to do this weekend!"

"This weekend?"

"Yes! This weekend! Our meeting is Monday after school!"

The orange flyer flashes before my eyes. FENCING FOR ALL.

"What's wrong?"

"Nothing!"

"You don't have something *better* to do on Monday, do you?"

She saw the flyer. She knows what's happening on Monday. She could have scheduled our meeting for literally any other day.

This is a test.

Or a trap.

"Ella!"

"What time is the meeting?" I ask.

Maybe I can still make the tournament. Morgan does travel soccer and horseback riding and hip-hop dance and attends fancy events with her very important parents and still finds time for Morgan & Ella business. Why can't I at least try to keep up with fencing *and* the brand?

"Four thirty," she says. "We'll have just enough time to get out of school and get our looks together before Izzy drives us . . ."

Four thirty. The same time as the tournament. Well, there goes that option. Not that it was ever *really* an option. There's no way Morgan would ever let me do both.

"Ribot Entertainment will take us to the next level of fame and fortune and followers!" Morgan promises. "So you better not blow it. You need to spend all weekend with me prepping for this audition like *nothing* you've ever prepped for before."

This is a one in a millionbilliontrillion opportunity. I know I should be, like, *electrified* with excitement right now. But I'm feeling oddly numb all over, like it's not really happening to me.

"Don't say anything to your mom until I've handled it," Morgan insists.

I don't know what she means by this, but I'm still flooded with relief. For once Morgan is making a demand that's super-easy to keep.

"What was all that shouting about?" Mom asks after I hang up.

"Oh, you know," I say. "Silly social media stuff."

Mom clucks her tongue but doesn't say another word, just as I knew she wouldn't.

OPPO RESEARCH

WHEN I ARRIVE AT SCHOOL, IT'S CLEAR THAT NEWS of our big meeting has already hit all the socials. I'm not surprised when Paisley is the first to rush up to congratulate me. Only she doesn't actually congratulate me.

"I have something to talk to you about," she whispers, looking around nervously. "Only I can't talk to you right now. Too many witnesses."

"Okaaaay."

"We'll talk in private after school," she says, "somewhere Morgan will never, ever go."

"Morgan? What does this have to do with Morgan?"

This is a ridiculous question. Morgan has *something* to do with *everything*.

"Shhh! You'll find out later. Just meet us in the library after last period."

"Us?" I ask. "Who is us?"

"Maddy and me."

"You and Maddy? Since when are you friends?"

"Since Morgan replaced her with Kaytee," Paisley says, "and she started eating lunch in the Digital Citizenship room."

My head is spinning.

"Look, I know this is a lot to take in, but you have to trust us," Paisley says. "Until then, just act normal!"

I try to act as oxymoronically normal as possible for the rest of the day, but it's impossible because there's nothing normal about the rest of this day. It seems like the whole school already knows about our audition—even teachers. Morgan knows we've reached something called "maximum engagement" when even Mr. Schlosser congratulates us on our big break at the start of Digital Citizenship. Only Coach Stout gives me a very disappointed look—she knows what this means for the fencing tournament—but she doesn't try to talk me out of my decision. And I know it sounds strange but I kind of wish she had.

Sophie isn't on social media. If Harumi or Sofie-with-an-f told Sophie about the audition, she doesn't give any hint of caring one way or another.

I leave for the library as soon as last bell rings. Somehow Maddy and Paisley have already arrived before me. They are doing a terrible job at pretending to read an old copy of *American Girl* magazine.

"Okay," I say wearily. "What's this all ab—?"

"Shhhhhhhhhhhhh!" Paisley hushes.

The three of us creep-walk to the way-back periodicals corner of the library with all the encyclopedias and dictionaries no one has looked at since, like, Mom was my age. Paisley keeps a finger pressed to her mouth as Maddy checks between the stacks to make sure we are really alone. When she gets the thumbs-up from Maddy, Paisley finally speaks.

"You know I'm Morgan & Ella's biggest OMG, right?"

I nod.

"So it is with great sadness that I have to make this confession." Paisley takes my hands in hers. "I bought Morgan's fans!"

If she had said "I bought Morgan's baby teeth," I wouldn't have been more surprised.

"You *what*?"

"Remember when Morgan got five thousand fans in a week? That's because I bought them!"

"*Morgan* bought them," Maddy corrects her.

"Well, technically *I* bought them using money Morgan paid me," continues Paisley. "So it couldn't get traced back to her if anyone ever looked into it."

"Which didn't work," Maddy says, "because I totally traced it back to her when I looked into it."

I'm too stunned to speak. *This* is the Digital Citizenship project Maddy has been working on? I mean, I knew it was kind of suspicious for Morgan to get so many fans so fast. But I never imagined she'd pay someone to buy fans for her! After accusing *me* of cheating! I'm dumbstruck by the two-facedness of it all.

"Omigoddess!" Paisley exclaims. "I think we broke Ella!"

"I'm just . . ." I swirl my hands in the air to express what I can't verbalize.

"Morgan asked—I mean, *demanded*—I do it, but I refused," Maddy says.

"So she turned to someone she knew couldn't say no," Paisley says in a choked voice. "Your biggest fan."

"Then she turned on me," Maddy says, "because eventually Morgan turns on everyone when they aren't useful to her anymore."

"Like Kaytee," Paisley adds.

Kaytee was beyond excited about our big news and didn't seem to mind that Morgan had bypassed her mom's PR connections in the pursuit of fame and fortune and followers. In fact, she was so bouncy with excitement that Morgan told her to take it down "like, *infinity* notches." She's so on the outs that she doesn't even realize she's been ousted.

"Kaytee couldn't deliver on two major gimmes," Maddy explains.

"Number one: the PR stuff," says Paisley. "And number two: Alex."

"As it turns out, the Mystery Hottie prefers to remain a mystery," Maddy says with a slight smile. "At least to Morgan."

Maddy and Paisley aren't telling me anything I don't already know. And this is my chance to one-up them both by telling them what Alex *really* thinks of Morgan. I have a feeling, though, that this gossip would only stir up major drama for

227

Alex that he doesn't want or deserve. Sometimes the fullest truth causes more harm than good. Thankfully, the moment for total honesty passes quickly when Paisley throws her arms around me.

"I hope you can forgive me for betraying you! I knew it was wrong, and I felt bad about it right away, but you know Morgan is so hard to say no to."

I don't think there's anyone who knows this better than I do.

"Why are you telling me this now?" I ask.

Maddy and Paisley exchange a look that says, *Do you want to do it or should I?*

"Because this audition is bad news for you," Maddy says.

"As your biggest fan, I hate to say it," Paisley adds. "But it's true."

"But it's the best thing that's ever happened to our brand," I say. "I mean, it's Ribot Entertainment! It doesn't get more influential than that! How is that a bad thing?"

Maddy looks me right in the eye to make sure I'm giving her my fullest attention to the fullest truth.

"You're just the next girl Morgan is using to get ahead."

I burst out laughing. Until now, everything Maddy and Paisley were saying sounded absolutely believable. Terrible, but believable.

This is also terrible, but totally ridiculous.

"Why does she need me to get ahead?" I say. "She's the one with the powerful family, money, and connections, not me!"

"That's *why* she chose you," Maddy says. "Have you ever heard of oppo research?"

Of course I haven't.

"Middletons are winners, right?" Maddy says. "A key to winning is not only knowing your opponents' strengths and weaknesses, but your own. Politicians like her father do it all the time. So Morgan will target her own negatives and turn them into positives before anyone else can take her down."

"Like the Love the Skin You're In video," Paisley offers. "Remember that one? When Morgan compared her legs to fluorescent light bulbs and said she was embracing the pasty?"

I don't remember this video at all. Paisley is way, waaaaaaay more familiar with Morgan & Ella's content than I am.

"She was pointing out her flaws to make girls feel better about themselves . . ."

"Ha!" Maddy laughs so loudly we get a quick shush from the librarian.

"Morgan doesn't care about making anyone feel better but herself!" Maddy whisper-shouts. "It's all *strategy*. I told her how my research showed it wouldn't be enough for you to be *aesthetic* and *multitalented* and *uplifting*. You also have to be *relatable role models*." She takes a deep breath then keeps going. "Anyway, one of Morgan's biggest flaws is that she's, like, not at all relatable, you know? Too out of touch with normals who don't live in mansions with congressman daddies. So what better way to prove your realness? Partnering up with the *realest* of girls."

Paisley is gazing at Maddy with stars in her eyes.

"I'm so sorry the OMGs never gave you the credit you deserve as the genius behind Morgan & Ella's success." Then Paisley slaps a hand to her mouth. "No offense, Ella! I mean, you're supertalented too . . ."

Absolutely none taken. All along Maddy was the brains of the operation. Morgan took what she needed and dumped her when she wasn't useful anymore.

Like she's doing to Kaytee.

And will eventually do to me?

"Has she nicknamed you yet?" Paisley asks.

"No," I reply. "At least I don't think so."

"When she gives you a nickname, that's when you know you're"—Maddy pauses for emphasis—"*Dunzo.*"

As further evidence, Maddy holds up her phone to show me an unflattering picture of Kaytee from Fotobomb that she screencapped before it disappeared. Kaytee was caught mid-mouthful and mid-blink, like she's more asleep than awake. Under the photo, another nickname to put on the latest tombstone in the cemetery of Morgan's dead friendships.

#FlakyKaytee

TEA PARTY

I'M LOOKING FORWARD TO BEING IN THE EMPTY apartment to process what Paisley and Maddy have told me. I need to prepare how I'm going to tell Morgan that I'm going ahead with the fencing tournament. If she really values me as a partner, she can simply reschedule our meeting for any other day. That's not too much to ask for, right? So I'm, like, double shook to interrupt a tea party in progress.

"Hi, Ella!" says Morgan.

"Hi, Ella!" says Mom.

Morgan.

And.

Mom.

Mom!

And!

Morgan!

And they've been together long enough to finish half cups of tea and start a sleeve of Thin Mints.

"Why are you here?"

The question is for both of them.

"Remember when I told you I was taking a half day today so I could study for my exam?" Mom says.

Obviously I do not remember this.

"Your mom does *such* important work," Morgan gushes. "I was telling her all about how my grandpa had a stroke and lost the use of his arm." She pauses to nod at Mom. "But after rehabilitation with his occupational therapist, he's back on the golf course!"

I don't want to hear another word of this heartwarming and possibly even true story.

"Why. Are. You. Here?"

It comes out more accusatory and less casual than I want it to.

"I could ask you the opposite question," Morgan says in a teasing voice. "Why *weren't* you here?"

"Yes, I was wondering the same thing," Mom says. "You're supposed to come home right after school every day. So imagine my surprise to come home to an empty apartment."

"I was at the library," I say truthfully. "Getting information. For a project."

"Really?" Morgan raises an eyebrow. "What project? For what class?" She turns to Mom. "Ella and I are in a lot of the same classes together except foreign language, math, science, and weirdly, gym. It's too late to switch to Mandarin. And Ella may never be an athlete like Lauren, so gym might be a hopeless case. But I think maybe with the right study skills she can get into the accelerated math and science with me . . ."

"I've always thought the same thing," Mom says.

"I'm always offering to be her study buddy, but she turns me down," Morgan says with a little pout.

Morgan excels in many areas:

School

Singing

Soccer

Hip-Hop

Horses.

But this—saying whatever needs to be said to get whatever she wants—is Morgan's greatest talent. And I am witnessing a virtuoso performance.

"Anyway, enough about all that!" Morgan says with a flick of her wrist. "I can't believe you didn't tell your mom about our meeting with Ribot Entertainment!"

But you told me not to tell her! I want to protest. *Until you handled it.*

And then I realize that this is Morgan "handling it." Right here, right now.

"I can't believe you didn't tell me either," Mom says, stretching her skeptical eyebrows to new forehead-climbing heights.

"I—" I stammer. "I—"

"Don't get mad at Ella, Ms. Plaza," Morgan says soothingly.

"I don't think she believes it's really happening. She's still in shock."

Those statements are 100 percent true and *truer*.

"And who can blame her?" Morgan continues. "I mean, this is an incredible, once-in-a-lifetime opportunity!"

"Morgan has gone to a lot of trouble to break it all down for me," Mom says.

Only then do I notice the binder on her place mat. It's not a study guide for anatomy class but a document titled "Morgan & Ella: A Guide to Global Multiplatform Domination."

"I knew your mom would have a lot of questions and concerns, so I put this together," Morgan says. "As you can see, it's everything she needs to know about our meeting and so much more."

I flip through the pages. As promised, the binder includes info we need for Monday, including bios on every key member of Riley Quick's management team and directions to their Manhattan office. It also contains a five-year social media campaign strategy, target promotional partnerships, and potential tour dates and cities.

"Morgan is very thorough," Mom says.

"And it all starts tomorrow night at our sleepover strategy session at Morgan & Ella HQ!"

"A sleepover?" I ask.

This invitation is a big deal. I've never been invited to stay overnight at the Middleton Mansion. And that never really bothered me because I'm not a huge fan of sleepovers. Truth is, I have trouble falling asleep in any bed that's not my own. My bedroom makes Morgan claustrophobic, but to me it's comforting—especially when Lauren is sleeping in the other bed. She used to make fun of me for being afraid of the dark—a big sister taunt that stung harder than most because it wasn't completely untrue. There's only one other house where I slept soundly and unafraid—dozens, if not hundreds, of times—next to my best friend in a sleeping bag on the floor.

But not anymore.

Morgan taps her spoon against the teacup to get my attention.

"Ella! Are you even listening to me?"

I am not.

"It will be so nice for you to hang out with Sophie again," Mom says.

"Sophie?!"

"Sophie!"

Mom sounds far more excited about me seeing Sophie than meeting Riley Quick's management team.

"What does Sophie have to do with this?" I ask.

"I invited Sophie to the sleepover."

Like polynomials, my brain simply cannot factor this outcome.

"You invited *Sophie*?!"

"I want to make the New Girl, Kaytee, feel welcome," Morgan says.

"You invited *Kaytee*? But I thought that whole family was can—"

Morgan cuts me off.

"Of course I invited Kaytee! And any friend of Kaytee's is a friend of mine! They can contribute valuable feedback for our audition . . ."

This is truly a master at work. Because absolutely nothing could be further from the truth. I thought I was hopelessly lost in pre-algebra, but I could not possibly be more confused than I am right now.

"I've been encouraging her to hang out with Sophie all year," Mom says to Morgan. "Maybe she can sing along in one of your videos. Wouldn't that be nice?"

Morgan sips her tea, then dabs her lips with a napkin before replying.

"It *would* be nice. But you know how *shy* Sophie can be. But with the right encouragement, maybe Ella and I can bring her out of her shell . . ."

A horn honks outside.

"Yikes! That's Izzy! I gotta go!" Morgan hops up and shakes Mom's hand. "It was so great to finally meet you, Ms. Plaza."

"You too, Morgan," Mom replies evenly.

The apartment door has barely closed behind us when Morgan is literally patting herself on the back. Again.

"And that is how it's done!"

"What happened in there?"

"I was winning over your mother," Morgan says in a self-congratulatory tone. "That's what."

"But why now?"

"Why now? Why *now*?" Morgan double ding-dongs her head. "This meeting is the most important thing that has ever happened to me!"

"Us," I correct.

"Us." Morgan takes me by both shoulders. *"Exactly."*

Her nails dig through the thin fabric of my T-shirt, straight through the skin.

"Ow!"

Morgan laughs likes I'm joking, but I'm not. Her manicure will definitely leave a mark.

"I need you to be your very best on Monday. We need intense practice if we're going to nail that audition. And this sleepover is, like, Morgan & Ella boot camp. I know Mama Plaza is not on board with our brand yet—even after reading my prospectus—so I invited Ickface to guarantee I'd get her on my good side . . ."

"You *really* invited Sophie to sleep over at your house?"

"Well, technically Kaytee invited her, and I gave my approval."

"But *why*?"

Morgan clenches and unclenches her fists.

"Kaytee had the nerve to give me an ultimatum! An ultimatum! Can you believe the New Girl's nerve? Said she'd come only if Sophie came."

"But why Kaytee? I thought she was canceled."

"We need *someone* to film all our behind-the-scenes content for Fotobomb! And Maddy is acting all petty and won't reply to my texts, so what other choice did I have? I've been put in a really awkward position, and I don't appreciate it, especially at such a crucial juncture in our career."

If anyone's in an awkward position it's Sophie. But it's asking far too much of Morgan to recognize that.

"But there's no way Ickface will actually show up. That's the upside to this *disaster*. I'll still get major credit with your Mama Plaza for being so kind, and she'll get on board with our brand, and you will nail the audition because you've *finally* got your Mom's full support . . ."

Izzy honks the horn again.

"Gotta go! I'm meeting with a personal shopper to put together a collection of audition outfits to choose from . . ."

She's halfway to the car before I call out what should be the obvious.

"Shouldn't I come with you?" I ask. "To pick out my own look?"

To which Morgan replies cheerfully and succinctly.

"Nope!"

When I go back inside, Mom is rinsing the teacups and saucers in the sink.

"You're sure you're okay with all this?" I ask. "I mean, this audition could change all our lives . . . ?"

"Isn't that what you want?" Mom asks with her back still to me.

Is it? Mom turns around and I hope that she'll see me like Lauren always says she does, all the way down to my soul. I hope she'll provide an answer to my own question.

"I'm more than okay with all this," she says. "I *insist*."

I always thought it was impossible to get anything past Mom. But I guess she met her match in Morgan Middleton. Mom's trusting response makes me feel a little less stupid about my own gullibility.

But not any smarter.

Which makes total sense for a Goofball, I guess. Only a fool would've thought I could convince Morgan to reschedule the biggest thing that's ever happened to her to avoid a conflict that only matters to me.

THE LAST CLASS

I'M NOT EXPECTED AT MIDDLETON MANSION UNTIL six p.m., which means I am totally free to attend my final fencing class.

I don't want to go.

What's the point? I'm not competing in the tournament, and I can't afford any more lessons, so why be reminded of how good I could have been if only I'd had the opportunity to get better?

But then I think about the fifty dollars Lauren paid for me to be there. One skipped class equals twelve dollars and fifty cents.

Twelve dollars and fifty cents doesn't sound like a lot. But I know the work that went into earning it. Twelve dollars and fifty cents equals one and a quarter lawns mowed. Fifty minutes of tutoring. Two and a half scoreless toddler soccer games.

So I show up for my final fencing lesson because that's the

responsible thing to do, even though I dread seeing Dede. She's not a fan of Riley Quick—she's really into rap—but even she has to understand why a meeting with Ribot Entertainment is a can't-miss opportunity, right?

But Dede surprises me by not even bringing it up.

"No time for talking today," she says. "Let's fence!"

So we spend the last class squaring off against one another in short bouts lasting three minutes or five touches, whichever comes first. So over the next nine minutes, I watch D.J. beat Jennifer, then Bob beat Julie, and Gilda beat Heather. It's actually pretty fun to watch, because everyone is on the same basic level. The competitors are evenly matched.

Until it's my turn.

It takes thirty-six seconds for me to get five touches on D.J.

It takes twenty-two seconds for me to get five touches on Bob.

It takes seventeen seconds for me to get five touches on Gilda.

I don't want to brag, but I seriously think the only way I could have possibly lost is if I'd had both arms tied behind my back. But my matches are not nearly as fun to watch because they are not even close. There's no tension or suspense.

And very little sense of accomplishment.

The class congratulates me on my victories. Half of them will be moving on to the next level. The Moms decided a pottery class is a better use of their "me time." But D.J., Bob, and Gilda have registered for the three-month-long beginners' class. I wish I could join them.

Actually, that's not totally true.

I want to go up against someone more skilled than they are. More skilled than me.

I want a challenge.

"Well, Ella," Dede says as she collects my helmet and chest guard, "it was nice having you in class."

I wait for Dede to give one last pitch for the tournament. But I'm surprised when she continues wiping down the equipment without saying another word.

"So that's it?" I ask. "You're not going to talk me into going to the tournament?"

Dede offers me a slight smile.

"It's not my job to talk you into anything," she says. "I can coach. I can encourage. But only you can decide to make fencing a priority."

"I want to," I protest, "but . . ."

But it's not up to me, I think.

"Thanks for everything, Dede," I say instead.

I walk out the door for the last time, expecting to see Alex, but he isn't there. I guess his class hasn't finished yet, so I peek through the window to catch a glimpse of him in action. His arms are out to the sides as he spins on one foot, with his other foot jutting out like a triangle from the knee of his supporting leg. He's

quick

graceful

and

precise.

Just like me.

I don't know when I'll see him again. I figure the least I can do is stick around long enough to say goodbye. When the class is over, he opens the door and lets everyone exit before he does.

"Hey," I say, trying to act casual.

"Hey," he says back with a grin that comes naturally to him.

"You were really good in there," I say.

"Thanks," he says. "Wish I could say the same about you. But I've never seen you fence, so I'd be lying."

His joke falls flat. It's not his fault though. He doesn't know the situation.

"You'll never get a chance to see me because today was my last class," I say. "Ever."

He holds the door open, and I step through it.

"Oh," he says. "But if your big meeting with Ribot Entertainment goes well, you'll get rich enough to take all the fencing classes you want."

"Wait!" I grab him by the arm. "You know about my meeting?"

I've sort of convinced myself that Alex only knows as much about me as I've told him myself. I hadn't counted on him following all the online gossip that continues to exist with or without my participation—or permission.

"Of course I know about your meeting! Kaytee told me all about it. She's more of a Kayter than a Ribot, but she's excited for you."

Well, I guess it's some consolation that he found out from his sister, not the socials. And I don't doubt that he's telling the truth. Overall, Kaytee is the most positive person I've ever met, even more than Paisley, whose enthusiasm is limited to her pop cultural obsessions.

"Even if the meeting goes well and I get rich," I say, "I still won't be able to take fencing classes."

"Why not?"

"Because fencing is off-brand."

"Says who?"

"Says Morgan."

Alex groans at the mention of her name.

"Do you think ballet class is *on-brand* for me?"

I sort of see his point. Alex is the last person I would've pictured doing pliés and pirouettes in his free time. But it's not the same thing. He's not seeking global multiplatform domination.

"You're not a brand," I say. "You're just you."

Alex stops in his tracks. His eyes grab mine, and hold on. The look he's giving me is something between a gaze and a glare—pity and disapproval. If I wasn't one of the foolish girls before, there's no doubt in my mind that he sees me that way now.

"When did you stop being you?"

Then he dashes away, leaving me alone on the sidewalk to give his deep question a simple answer:

I stopped being me when Morgan started telling me exactly what to wear, post, link, sing, say, and think.

Or is that a deep answer to a simple question?

ORIGIN STORY

I'VE BEEN TO MIDDLETON MANSION MANY TIMES, and it never gets any less bizarre to me that someone actually lives here. It's grand and foreboding and has an actual tower called a turret, a word I'm familiar with from the Dragonologist Chronicles. Any day now they'll install a moat filled with laser dolphins.

When Morgan greets me with an enthusiastic hug, I'm thinking maybe Maddy and Paisley are wrong. Morgan really likes me for who I am and not what she thinks I can do for her image.

"Omigoddess! We have so much to do!"

I follow Morgan through one enormous living room before passing through what I think is a *second* enormous living room—or maybe it's the family room? Media room? Great room? There are a lot of enormous rooms to keep track of and they're all full of oversized earth-toned furniture that somehow all looks the same. Whatever room we're in, Morgan hangs a left and starts making her way up a marble staircase to Morgan & Ella HQ on the second floor.

As always, Morgan spreads out on a skinny, zebra-striped couch called a divan. I usually flop into a beanbag at her feet, but for now I'm more comfortable standing. Morgan takes notice, because Morgan notices everything.

"Have a seat," she says, gesturing to the floor. "Relax."

"I'm good," I say, before quickly moving on to business. "So what do you want to do first?"

Morgan watches me carefully, clearly debating whether to make an issue of my decision to stand. When she smiles at me, I know she's letting it go.

"So before we work on our songs, our look, or anything else," Morgan says, "we have to work on our story."

"Our story?" I ask. "What story?"

"About how Morgan & Ella came to be," she says. "Our origin story."

"Well, that *technically* wouldn't be an origin story," I say, "because we're not, like, heroes or villains . . ."

"Oh, I'm *sorry*," Morgan says. "I forgot what a book lover you are. Maybe when Ickface gets here we can forget all about preparing for the biggest audition of our lives and just sit around eating junk food and reading the Dragonologist Chronicles all night. Would you like that instead?"

"Well . . ."

"Well, *what?*"

"Doesn't it make more sense for us to postpone the audition so we can really perfect our sound and aesthetics? What's the rush?"

It's an honest suggestion. If we reschedule, I'll be better prepared to impress. Nailing this audition benefits both of us. Getting to participate in the tournament is an added bonus. Why should Morgan be the only one who gets everything she wants?

"What's the rush?" Morgan mimics me perfectly. "We're already losing fans to the competition!"

"What competition?"

"EVERYONE WHO IS NOT US."

Morgan is literally pulling her hair out. Just when I think she's on the verge of a total meltdown, she closes her eyes, brings prayer hands up to her face, and takes a deep breath. It's a popular Fotobomb pose.

#zen #peace #blessed

And maybe it actually works because when she opens her eyes, her face is calm again.

"Our origin story," she says, as if this line of conversation hadn't been broken. "You can thank me for already turning your weakness into a strength."

"What weakness?" I manage to ask. "Into what strength?"

She levels me with the Girlbossiest of looks.

"Your deadbeat dad," she says. "Our unlikely friendship."

I'm stunned. Not by what she has said, but how easily she said it.

"You'll tell everyone how my family has become your family," Morgan says. "And the congressman has become, like, a father figure to you."

I'm so happy I didn't flop into the beanbag. It's much harder to make a stand sitting down.

"I may not have a dad, but I already have a family," I say firmly. "And I've never even met your father."

"We can make an effort to correct that," she says.

"So what? I'll have breakfast with the congressman tomorrow morning and—BAM!—he's my replacement daddy?"

When she doesn't deny it, I know for sure that's exactly what Morgan has in mind.

"This narrative really is the best option," Morgan insists.

"For who?" I ask.

"For Morgan & Ella!"

"For Morgan & Ella," I repeat softly.

I think about Paisley and Maddy's warnings. That Morgan Middleton is never, ever in it for anyone but herself. If I don't ask this question right now, I know I'll regret it.

"Why do you even need me?"

Morgan blinks slowly.

"What do you mean?"

"You could just go solo," I say, "and not have to worry about my messy background bringing you down."

"You don't get it," Morgan says. "Your messy background lifts me up!"

What did Maddy say about Morgan's biggest flaws? That picking me made her—and her family—appear more real?

She stretches herself out on the divan like royalty.

"When Daddy runs for president—"

She's right in front of me, but I swear I mishear her.

"What?"

"When Daddy," she repeats with emphasis, *"runs for president—"*

"President of what?"

"The United States."

"Your father is running for president of the United States?!"

"Not *now*," she responds casually, "but, like, eventually."

Congressman Middleton will be master of the universe, like, *eventually* in the same way my mom will get her master's degree, like, *eventually*.

"When it's time for him to choose a running mate," Morgan continues, "he can't choose someone who's too much like him, even though he's brilliant. The veep has to make the president look good. And if the veep is too brilliant, like the president, everyone will compare them to each other all the time. And the veep could actually overshadow the guy in charge. So Daddy has to pick someone who is different enough, but not so different that they drag the ticket down."

I'm only sort of understanding why she's telling me this.

"I'm like the veep?" I ask. "My job is to look good but not *too* good?"

"Your job," Morgan replies, "is to make Morgan & Ella look good."

Which is why Morgan tells me exactly what to wear, post, link, sing, say, and . . .

"*That's* how you bring the perfect balance to my brand."

Suddenly, the most ridiculous of Maddy and Paisley's claims—that Morgan needs me as much as I need her—seems not ridiculous in the least.

"*Our* brand," I correct her.

"Duh!" She ding-dongs her head. "Of course! *Ours!* That's what I said!"

"But it isn't what you said," I reply. "And it isn't what you think either."

Morgan's smile vanishes quicker than a deleted selfie.

"Why are you giving me such attitude right now? Do I need to remind you of everything I've done to get you here? You were a disaster when we first met, Ella. A *disaster*. You have no idea how uncute you were before I gave you clothes and makeup and—omigoddess!—you'd never even had a *manicure* before you met me! And now you've got a meeting with Riley Quick's management team! Which means you're, like, destined to one day meet Riley Quick herself! It's a dream come true! Don't you want the best life for you and your mom and your sister?"

"Of course I want what's best, but . . ."

"But nothing! You're acting like an ungrateful . . ."

The end of her rant is lost in a groan.

"Ughhhhhh. I can't believe it." She points to the security monitor. "Ickface has arrived."

Omigoddess. I can't believe it either. Sophie actually showed up.

And I've never, ever been happier to see someone who isn't speaking to me.

SUCKERELLA

SOPHIE STANDS AS STILL AS THE LION STATUES guarding the entrance to Middleton Mansion. I don't blame her for being too timid—or intimidated?—to ring the doorbell.

"Are you just going to stand here all night?" Morgan asks as a greeting.

"Hey, Soph," I say. "Saw you on the security cam."

"Hey," she replies.

Morgan obviously does not want her here. So it falls to me to make her feel welcome. Not out of politeness, I realize. But for my own protection.

Now that Sophie's here, I don't want her to leave.

"Come in," I say, even though it's Morgan's house.

She grips the handle to her rolling suitcase. It's the same one my mom always complimented her on for having "smart ergonomics."

"You'll have the strongest spine of all of us," Mom would say.

She already does.

This has never been truer than right now, as Sophie—source of a million meanie memes, a billion Fotobomb burns, and a trillion trolling hashtags—steps bravely inside the unwelcoming entrance to Middleton Mansion, pulling her memeable, burnable, hashtaggable rolling suitcase behind her.

"Okay, I just told Izzy not to bother us because we're filming," Morgan says. "Maybe this time she won't ruin our best take by offering us *snacks*."

"Kaytee should be here soon, right?" Sophie asks.

I wanted to ask the same question. Again, she's got a stronger spine than I do.

"Oh, you don't know?" Morgan snarks. "I thought you two were *besties*."

Morgan holds on to the moment for maximum tension.

"She bailed on us about an hour ago. Said she wasn't feeling well after the game."

"Kaytee's really not coming?" I ask.

"Nope."

She probably didn't find #FlakyKaytee very funny.

I think it. But I don't say it.

"And *your* bestie is here instead," Morgan continues. "Funny how that worked out, huh? It's downright *hilarious*."

Morgan says it like the least hilarious joke ever told.

"What about Maddy?" Sophie asks.

"Dunzo? Don't talk to me about Dunzo."

This news comes as a shock to Sophie. That's how little she pays attention to the popularity hierarchy at Mercer Middle School.

"It's just the three of us?" Sophie gulps. "All night?"

"Yeah," Morgan sighs, opening the door to her bedroom. "And *you* are going to make yourself useful."

Sophie's huge eyes aren't big enough to take in all the bling and bedazzle, pinks and purples, predator and prey animal prints. I almost laugh because it's exactly the look I must've had on my face when I saw Morgan's room for the first time.

"Let's not waste any time," Morgan says to me. "Grab your ukulele, and let's get this thing done."

"What do I do?" Sophie asks.

"You wait for me to tell you what to do!"

I honestly don't understand why Sophie is still here. If I were her, I would've hopped on my bike and pedaled myself as far away from this place as possible.

I'm not even her, and that still seems like a tempting option.

Morgan just assumes I've perfected the Riley Quick song she decided will best reflect our aesthetic at the audition. "Red Lips, Black Heart" was the first song I ever taught myself on the ukulele. I can play it in my sleep.

Unfortunately, Morgan cannot sing it wide-awake.

Okay, to be totally fair, it's not all her fault. It's three-part harmony, and there's only two of us. The middle of the chord is missing, so Morgan's lead sounds totally out of tune. Especially on the pre-chorus that goes:

There's not enough makeup
to make up
for the ugliness
on your two faces . . .

After the third unsuccessful take, Morgan loses it.

"I'm reapplying my mascara," she says. "And when I get back, you better be ready to sing in tune, Suckerella!"

Suckerella.

Morgan's word.

Suckerella.

Morgan's sword.

Sucker. Ella.

Plunges directly.

Sucker.

Into the light-up target.

Ella.

That once was my heart.

Suckerella.

It rolls so easily off her tongue. This is not the first time she's said it out loud. Just the first time she's said it straight to my face.

When she gives you a nickname, Maddy warned, *that's when you know you're Dunzo.*

How fitting that Sophie of all girls is here to witness my cruel demotion to future memedom.

Sophie gently places a hand on mine.

"It's not your fault," she whispers.

I'm almost furious with Sophie for being so nice to me. I don't deserve her kindness or comfort. Maybe I never did.

"I know that!" I shoot back. "The middle harmony is missing!"

And she's wrong. It's my fault that she's even here! And there's nothing I can do to make it better . . .

"Mmmmmmmm . . ."

Sophie hums the middle harmony to herself. Her eyes are closed, and her lips are turned in on themselves, and she doesn't even know she's doing it. It's this totally unconscious, unflattering expression that earned the nickname I have never used.

Will never use.

"Mmmmmmmm . . ."

She's perfectly on key.

"Maybe," I suggest cautiously, "you could fill it in?"

It really would sound so much better if Morgan would give Sophie a chance to sing with us. She can hit all the highest notes, and she's also much better at blending than Morgan. She might lack Morgan's on-camera charisma, but I bet that could come with compliments. And confidence.

"Maybe," Sophie says.

Morgan has returned with spidery eyes.

There's not enough makeup
to make up
for the ugliness
on your two faces . . .

I give Sophie an encouraging nod.

"So, Morgan," she says, "I was thinking . . ."

"If I wanted to know what you were thinking," Morgan snaps, "I'd ask."

"Well, actually, *we* were thinking," I say, surprising myself—and Sophie—with my use of the inclusive pronoun, "that the harmony would come together if Sophie sang the middle part . . ."

Morgan stops me before I get any further.

"You want to introduce Ickface to Ribot Entertainment? You're kidding me!" She levels a lethal gaze at me, then back at Sophie. "No, you're *killing* me!"

I mouth *I'm sorry* when Morgan's back is turned. But Sophie misses it, too, because she dashes into the bathroom, which, really, is okay, because my silent apology is so overdue and so inadequate that I immediately want to take it back anyway. I'm sorry for so much more than what's happening right here and now in Morgan & Ella headquarters.

I'm sorry.

I'm sorry I wasn't a better friend.

I'm sorry I wasn't a better friend and didn't speak up.

I'm sorry I wasn't a better friend and didn't speak up when Morgan brought you down . . .

Why don't I have the courage to say it out loud? Is it because I'm afraid Sophie won't accept my apology?

"I'll never forgive Kaytee for sticking us with Ickface

tonight," Morgan huffs. "I should've known Flaky would bail. She thinks she's so special because she's the only seventh grader on the travel soccer team now."

"Wait . . . What do you mean?"

Morgan dusts her shoulders off.

"I quit."

"You did *what*? *When?*"

"Today. Effective immediately."

"You *quit*? But why? I thought Middletons weren't quitters."

"We're not! We're winners! And I'm fully committing myself to the brand! I won't have time for travel soccer when I'm on tour!" she says. "I don't expect anything less from you!"

"But I thought *doing it all* was all a part of being a Girlboss . . ."

"It still is," Morgan explains, "but priorities change. And Morgan & Ella is far more important to me than any soccer team that's oh-and-three this season. I mean, if we were undefeated, maaaaaaybe I'd make it work. You know, just to show the world how totally normal I still am. But I don't have time to waste with *losers*."

The toilet flushes, and Sophie re-emerges looking pale and unwell.

"Perfect timing," Morgan says with a sneer.

"I feel sick," Sophie says. "I want to go home."

Same, I think. *Same.*

But only one of us grabs her suitcase.

"Maybe you and Kaytee have come down with the same thing," Morgan muses. "Loseritis."

Only one of us walks out.

Morgan follows Sophie just to make sure she doesn't get lost on her way out. I stay put because I don't need to see or hear any more than I already have.

"Well, this worked out even more perfectly than I planned!" Morgan says triumphantly when she comes back. "Ickface is gone, Dunzo is gone, Flaky is gone. It's just you and me, Morgan & Ella, ready to take over the world! Though it's totally annoying that we can't do a multicam edit of all the behind-the-scenes prep for our audition." She pauses for a second to scroll through her messages. "Omigoddess! I have an idea! Why don't *you* film me behind the scenes? Girlboss Lessons is blowing up lately and—"

She stops midsentence and gasps at her phone.

"What is the meaning of this?"

She shoves the screen too close to my eyes to see anything but a blur.

"You? And Alex?"

So much for keeping our friendship a secret. An anonymous middle school paparazzo snapped photos of Alex and me as we walked home from the YMCA today. There's nothing incriminating about these photos at all, other than the fact that it shows Alex and me together without Morgan.

"There is no me and Alex," I say truthfully.

"Is this you?" She points at my face on the screen. "And Alex?"

"Yes." I nod. "And yes."

"Well, that proves there is a you and Alex!"

She swipes at her phone to show shot after boring shot of Alex walking alongside me and my bike.

"I don't get it!" Morgan seethes. "I mean, you don't even look cute in these pictures!"

Whoever took these pictures captured the exact moment Alex asked the question: *When did you stop being you?*

"You knew how much I liked him and betrayed me by hanging out with him behind my back!"

"We weren't hanging out," I say. "We just happened to run into each other . . ."

I'm reluctant to explain myself because I don't want Alex dragged into this any more than he already has been. I want to do a better job at keeping his secret than I did my own. Whoever spied on us wants to drive a wedge between Morgan and me. Whoever took and sent these pictures wants to sabotage the meeting with Ribot Entertainment. It has to be Paisley and Maddy. But why? Are they really looking out for me? Or are they just jealous haters?

I don't know what or who to believe anymore. I watch Morgan's face for clues to what will happen next. I catch a rippling across her features—top to bottom, a softening of brows, nostrils, lips—as she makes the decision to have mercy on me.

"You're lucky I already canceled him and his whole family."

Morgan's voice is eerily calm now, as if she hadn't been in a full shout ten seconds ago.

"You're lucky I'm willing to put your betrayal behind me."

As if she hadn't called me "Suckerella" ten minutes ago.

"You're lucky I'm a professional who will not throw away *months* of hard work over a loser boy."

As if she hadn't been making a fool out of herself in front of this "loser boy" ten days ago.

Morgan pauses and I realize she's waiting for me to express gratitude for her forgiveness.

"Thank you, Morgan."

"And?"

"I'm sorry?"

Morgan nods. That was the right answer. But it's still not enough.

"I accept your apology," she says. "But can you swear to me right now that you'll never let any boy distract you again? That you're as committed to Morgan & Ella as I am? That you're all in?"

She's holds out her palm for me to take. This is no ordinary handshake. This is an oath of loyalty. If I refuse her hand, I'm rejecting the brand. I'll be giving up on fame, fortune, and followers—and all the free fashion, fancy manicures, and faboosh perks that go with it. And for what? To be ordinary instead of extraordinary, the pathetic, mostly-forgotten footnote in Morgan Middleton's bio.

But can I really promise to be as committed as she is?

"Omigoddess! Of course I am!"

This is the only acceptable answer, even if we both suspect it isn't true.

No one goes all in like Morgan Middleton.

THIS. IS. NOT. ME.

HEY, OMGS!

So this is Morgan's nan—I mean, assistant—driving us into Manhattan for our meeting with Ribot Entertainment! Izzy is taking us because Congressman Middleton is in Washington, DC, for a Very Important vote on a Very Important bill and Attorney Middleton is arguing a Very Important case in a Very Important courtroom. Morgan says they are Very Important people living Very Important lives. My mom also wanted to be here to support us, but she couldn't get the day off on such short notice and also she has a can't-miss exam tonight. When I tell Morgan that my mom is Very Important to her clients, she comes at me with a makeup brush saying, "You need to rethink your whole brow game."

I went to school but didn't say a word to anyone all day because I was on strict instructions from Morgan to rest my vocal chords. This prescription conveniently excused me from all awkward conversations and confrontations with girls claiming to be concerned friends and fans. Morgan skipped school to get her eyelashes tinted and she keeps blinking a lot, like she's being stabbed by a millionbilliontrillion tiny daggers in her pupils. So this is me asking if she is maybe having an allergic reaction to the dye because the whites of her eyes are kind of redder than usual, but she tells me to focus on myself and not mess this up for her—whoopsie!—she means us.

So this is me following Morgan into the lobby of this fancy building in Manhattan that is all marble and chrome and filled with Very Important people. We stop at the security desk, and Morgan informs the unsmiling woman behind the desk that we have a meeting with Ribot Entertainment, and part of me is hoping that the unsmiling woman will start cackling with laughter and turn us away because there's no way two twelve-year-olds could possibly have a meeting scheduled with Riley Quick's management team. But she confirms our appointment with the receptionist on the tenth floor and hands over our visitor badges and points a finger toward the bank of elevators that will take us there.

Yes, this is really happening.

This is me rising up, up, up in the elevator toward Morgan & Ella's destiny.

This is me wishing I hadn't drank a liter of tea on the car ride over, but Morgan insisted on hydration and vocal lubrication. When the doors part, my bladder feels like an overfilled water balloon.

This is Morgan asking me if I'm ready for my life to change.

This is me telling Morgan I have to pee.

This is Morgan telling me to pull myself together.

This is Morgan lecturing me on professionalism or lack thereof.

This is Morgan telling me that her eyeballs feel like beehives but I don't see her complaining, now do I?

This is Morgan furious at bodily functions.

This is Morgan unsatisfied with telling me what to wear, post, link, sing, say, and think; she wants to control how I pee.

This is me wondering if there's any limit to the ways Morgan can get mad at me for being me.

PICS OR IT DIDN'T HAPPEN

I'M PEEING AS QUICKLY AS POSSIBLE SO I CAN GET back to the biggest meeting of Morgan Middleton's life. Only after I've flushed and washed and dried my hands do I hear the whimpers and moans coming from the handicapped stall.

"I *(snurfle)* SHOULDA *(blurfle)* BEEN *(gurfle)* THERE . . ."

Normally, I would mind my own business. But whoever is in there sounds wounded. Like she needs help.

"Are you okay in there?" I ask.

snurfle blurfle gurfle

I don't know how to interpret these sounds.

"Um? Are you sure?"

"NOOOOOOOOO."

Then the metal lock unlatches and the bathroom door swings open to reveal a young woman hunched on the toilet seat. She's distraught and disheveled but still totally gorgeous. In fact, she looks *a lot* like Riley Quick . . .

OMG

THIS

SNURFLING

BLURFLING

GURFLING

GIRL

IS

RILEY

QUICK.

She's got one of the most famous faces in the world. I know it's her. And yet, this snurfling, blurfling, gurfling girl, curled up elbows on knees, head in hands, looks absolutely nothing like her.

"My Bee-Eff-Eff got married yesterday!" she sobs.

"Oh!" I reply. "Congratulations to her!"

"I wasn't invited."

She hangs her head low. I squat down so we're on the same level.

"Oh," I say. "I see."

She pops up.

"LOOK!"

She thrusts her phone in my face. It's a model so shiny and new it probably won't be available to the public for, like, another year or two. Free swag is one of the perks of being famous. But right now, these most technologically advanced, highest-quality images are making Riley Quick—OMG RILEY QUICK!!!—miserable.

"Look how happy Gabby is without me!"

Gabby . . . Mackenzie. Formerly of Mack & Quick, who chose an "ordinary, boring life" over global multiplatform domination.

Gabby Mackenzie, just a normal human being.

I guess Morgan's story wasn't totally bogus after all.

Riley Quick is scrolling through Fotobomb too fast for me to see anything but blurs of white dress and black suit and flowers and sunsets and . . .

"Aren't you supposed to be in Tokyo right now? On the Asian leg of your international tour? That's pretty cool too . . ."

She shrugs.

"I used to think so," she says. "Now I'm just . . . tired."

I'm exhausted by Morgan's Must-Dos and we've only got, like, twenty thousand fans? Riley Quick has at least ten thousand times more fans than we do. Is it possible to be ten thousand times as exhausted?

She looks it.

"I left my tour and flew here to tell my management team I'm done."

"Done?"

"I quit."

I lose my balance and fall backward onto the bathroom tile.

"Quit?" I yelp. "You can't quit! You're too important to girls like me!"

She smiles for the first time in our conversation. But it isn't the Riley Quick smile I'm so used to seeing in photos and videos. It's more reserved. More real.

"Not forever," she assures me. She starts scrolling through her phone again. After a few moments, she settles on an image. "Just long enough to remember why I got started in the first place."

She holds it up for me to see. Two girls with guitars. One with frizzy hair and a mouth full of braces. The other with freckles and a long black braid hanging over her shoulder.

Mack & Quick.

Riley Quick shakes her fingers through her straightened—but dull—hair. Her nail polish is chipped, the tips ragged. When she sits up, I get my first good look at what she's wearing.

"OMG!" I point at the image of FlutterFyre on her T-shirt. "You're a fan of the Dragonologist Chronicles?"

Riley Quick looks right at me with her famous violet eyes, and I swear she's put HydraCaster's most powerful enchantment spell on me.

"Totally!" she exclaims. "I've been obsessed with the series since I was about your age. I've had this shirt forever. It's like my security blanket, I guess. I wear it to sleep, but I'm never supposed to wear it out in public because it doesn't go with my"—she stops to squeeze air quotes with her fingers—"*brand*."

"Omigoddess! Me too! Everything you just said!"

Riley Quick does not look at all surprised by my reaction.

I think Riley Quick is very used to girls like me telling her that she's just like them. *That* is Riley Quick's brand. And I think this Everygirl image started out as the truth . . . until it got warped to the point where it's hard to tell what's fake and what's real, and okay, yeah, now I'm thinking more about myself than Riley Quick. Never, ever in a millionbillion-trillion years did I think I'd have so much in common with Riley Quick! I'm curious if she's a mixed-up in-betweener FlusterFlutter like me . . .

"Do you want a selfie?" she asks.

I can't believe any of this is happening. And if I don't record any evidence, no one—especially not Morgan—will believe me either.

And yet.

Riley Quick's face has changed again. Her smile is tighter now, and her eyes are sadder. She isn't a FlusterFlutter. The Cauldron of Serpentyne would definitely sort her with the ScaleShifters.

"No, thank you," I reply.

"Are you sure?" she asks. "Everyone always wants a selfie."

"I'm sure," I reply.

I have a feeling everyone wants something from Riley Quick. And I don't want to be everyone.

"Do you want a hug?" I ask.

International superstar Riley Quick's violet eyes expand to twice their size, like a super-sped-up time-lapse video of flowers in bloom.

"Yes," she says. "Yes, I do."

And now I've got not just my arms, but my whole heart and soul wrapped around Riley Quick. But in this moment, she isn't an international superstar or the number one followed person on Fotobomb. She's just a girl who messed up, who misses her best friend and is very, very sad because she may not be able to get her back into her life again.

She also smells incredible, like a freshly peeled grapefruit rolled in superfine sugar.

I decide I will never tell anyone about this hug. Not even if, like, after a year-long hiatus, Riley Quick bursts back onto the scene with her biggest and best song of her career, an international chart topper about a chance encounter in a toilet with an extraordinarily ordinary girl who reminded her why she started making music in the first place.

Which is fine because no one would ever believe me anyway.

Without pics, it never happened.

NO, I THINK

MORGAN IS PACING OUTSIDE THE ENTRANCE TO Ribot Entertainment. In one minute, we will be one minute late for the most important meeting of Morgan Middleton's life.

"Are you *finally* ready to prove you're all in and as committed to Morgan & Ella as I am?"

No, I think.

"No," I say out loud.

Morgan rattles her head around on her shoulders.

"What? Did? You? Say?"

"No."

The door opens, and a pink-haired hipster with thick, black glasses pops her head into the hall.

"Are you girls ready?"

I don't need to see the flash of Morgan's Everygirl smile to know this is a Very Important person.

"One minute!"

The door closes, Morgan's smile vanishes.

"Maybe you didn't hear me," she says. "I asked if you're as committed to Morgan & Ella as I am. And you're saying . . ."

"No," I repeat.

But there's so much more to that no.

No, I'm not as committed to Morgan & Ella as you are.

No, I don't want to go to the audition.

No, I don't want to be the other half of your brand.

No, I don't want global multiplatform domination.

No, I don't want to be memed, burned, or hashtagged.

No, I don't want Sophie, Kaytee, Maddy, or anyone else memed, burned, or hashtagged.

No, I'm not afraid of The Eyeroll.

No, I don't want anything to do with you anymore, Morgan Middleton.

But Morgan doesn't deserve to hear the fullest truth. I answer again, simply.

"No."

Would I have found this courage if I hadn't shared a chance encounter in a toilet with the biggest pop star in the world? I'll never know. I'd like to think so.

I pick up my ukulele and walk away from the most important meeting of Morgan Middleton's life. I take the elevator down, down, down and find Izzy waiting in the main lobby. Morgan won't chase me down—tryharding is not her style—but I'm desperate to get away.

"I want to go home, Izzy," I say. "Please take me home."

Her mouth turns down at the corners. "I'm sorry," she says. "I'm so sorry."

At first I think she's apologizing for her loyalty to Morgan. But when she pulls out her phone and calls me a car, I realize she's apologizing for so much more, in the same way my silent "sorry" to Sophie tried to make up for all the bad behavior that came before.

We don't live that far outside the city. On the map, my tiny apartment is so close to the Manhattan skyscraper where Morgan is probably pitching her Girlboss Lessons solo project to the pink-haired rep from Ribot Entertainment. And yet these two dropped pins are universes apart.

There's a lot of rush hour traffic, so the ride home takes a lot longer than the drive out. There's no hope for making it to the fencing tournament before it's over. I'm disappointed, of course. But if I've really got the talent Coach Stout and Dede see in me, I have to believe this won't be my last chance. Morgan always made it seem like we were running out of time for our big break. But I'm not even thirteen! I'm tired of singing other people's words. I've got so many unsung songs inside me.

"Universes Apart" would make a great title, I think.

THE FULLEST LOVE

IT'S A LITTLE AFTER SEVEN P.M. WHEN I UNLOCK the front door to the apartment. It's the magic hour after work and before class, and Mom is at her computer cramming for her test. I feel bad to burst in like this, but she seems relieved by the interruption.

"Izzy called me," she explains.

"I'm sorry," I say. "I needed to come home."

Mom turns away from the screen.

"I'm not surprised by that at all."

"You're not?"

"Nope." She gets up, then pushes aside pillows to make room for us on the couch. "I'm only surprised you lasted as long as you did."

Of all the confusing conversations I've had lately, this is definitely the confusingest.

"After sitting down to tea with Morgan," Mom says, "I saw for myself that she was even worse than I thought she was."

My mouth hangs open. Mom good-humoredly taps my chin to close it up.

"You were only pretending to like her?" I ask. "But why?"

"I had to let you see Morgan for who she really is," she says. "A manipulator. A con artist."

Morgan hadn't gotten one over on my mom after all.

Mom had gotten one over on me.

"I know you never approved of our *silly social media stuff*," I say. "But Morgan really made it seem possible that we'd get rich and famous together." I poke at a small hole in the pillow. "I wanted the best life not just for myself but so you didn't have to work so hard anymore."

Mom pulls me closer and I don't resist. I ease into her arms like I haven't done in a very, very long time. Too long.

"First of all, Ella, I *like* working hard," Mom says. "And second of all, any friendship built on becoming rich and famous is no friendship at all." She strokes my hair. "I can understand why you found Morgan so appealing. She introduced you to a whole world of power and privilege. And when she turns on the charm, she can make you feel like the most important person on the planet—well, besides herself, right? Because it's always going to be about Morgan Middleton. That's the trade-off with people like that. They make every day into an exhilarating adventure. It's fun at first, but after a while, all that drama gets exhausting. Especially when that person doesn't give you any genuine support in return for your loyalty."

I can't help but think Mom has had a lot of experience dealing with someone like this.

And it doesn't require a secret map to lead me to the right answer.

"I messed up, Mom," I say, my eyes welling with tears. "I made the wrong choice."

"I'm sorry you missed the tournament," she says.

That's not what I was talking about, but Mom doesn't give me a chance to correct her.

"Well, as a result of all my hard work, I got a raise," she says. "And I think with some budgeting, we can find enough money for these fencing lessons if it's that important to you . . ."

I'm too overcome with gratitude to let her finish.

"Yes! Yes! Yes! Thank you! Thank you! Thank you!"

Fencing is *that* important to me. Morgan Middleton made me forget who I was for a while. But when Dede handed me the foil for the first time, I started to find myself again. I throw my arms around Mom and weep into her shoulder. I can't remember the last time I cried in front of her, let alone *on* her.

"You're welcome, honey," she says, holding me tight. "But these aren't tears of joy, are they?"

"I made an even worse choice!" I yelp. "I dumped Sophie for Morgan and I think I want her back because she never stopped being The Best Friend in My Head!"

That last part makes no sense, but Mom seems to under-stand exactly what I mean.

"You messed up," she agrees. "And even if you ask for Sophie's forgiveness, you may not get it."

I let out another choked sob when she says this, because I know it's true.

Riley Quick knew it, too, about Gabby Mackenzie. And that's how someone with 200 million Fotobomb followers ends up sobbing in a toilet all alone.

"The best you can do is learn from this hurt you're feeling right now. Be a good friend in the future to those who have earned it."

Mom lets me rest my slobbery, snotty face into her shoulder until I feel better. If that isn't the fullest love, I don't know what is.

"You can get some practice right now by being a good sister," she says.

"Really? How?"

"Lolo needs to hear from you."

I don't ask why because part of me already knows. I want to be wrong about this like I'm wrong about so many other things. I want Lauren to be right about this like she is always right about everything.

REVEALING IS
HEALING

SHE PICKS UP ON THE FIRST RING.

"Lala."

"Lolo."

There's a muddy *thump-thump-thump* of bass in the background. A party happening somewhere, but my sister doesn't sound like she's in a festive state of mind.

"Our father," Lauren says, "isn't coming after all."

I'll never forget the song playing during this conversation. It's a fuzzy dubstep remix, but the message is loud and clear.

Stop concealing
Revealing is healing
Give me the fullest truth

"I'm sorry, Lala," I say.

"I'm the big sister!" She blows her nose. "I should be consoling you!"

"I never believed he'd actually come," I say. "He's bailed on you—on us—too many times before."

"He always wants to be the good guy but never follows through," Lauren says. "I should've known better than to fall for it." A pause. "Again."

She sniffles.

"Allergies," she says.

My sister has never suffered allergies. Or fools. Which is why this news is hitting her so hard.

"I think it's kind of beautiful that you still believe in him," I say. "You act like a cynic, but deep down you're a secret optimist."

"Secret Optimist" would make a great title, I think.

"Ha." It's a bitter, humorless laugh. "Isn't that your role in the family?"

"He never gave me a reason to believe in him," I say. "At least you have that."

Lauren just sighs.

"You said your soccer coach is tough on new recruits, right?"

"We hated her for making us do the same drills over and over and over again," Lauren replies. "But she was breaking us down to build us up. Now we're all stronger than ever before."

I let her words sink in for a few seconds.

"It's just like the calluses on my fingers from practicing the ukulele or how my fencing instructor won't let me beat her in bouts," I say. "It's just like *life.*"

Lauren laughs again, only this time there's some joy in it.

"Who gave you permission to be the wise sister?"

"Well," I say, "I learned from the best."

THIS IS REALLY ME

HEY, FRIENDS!

First, I want to thank you all for your support. My friend Paisley reads through every single one of your messages and shares the best ones with me. I'm much happier in this mostly offline life. Mom always said there were advantages to growing up as a seventh grader in the nineties, and I guess she was right. I hear more clearly when I'm looking at a face instead of a phone. And I'm less distracted in class when I'm not worrying about what's blowing up on Fotobomb. Maybe you should try it too?

Ha! Funny advice from someone making an online video, huh?

I'm here only because I want to say I'm sorry if you're sad about the end of Morgan & Ella. Paisley helped me understand that our posts and videos were important to a lot of you and that it would be kind of rude to just disappear without a proper goodbye. I mean, if you're bothering to watch me sit here and babble to a camera, then I know you must really care!

So yes, it's true that I'm responsible for deleting our socials—thank you, Maddy, for your techy expertise. There was just too much negativity I didn't want to be associated with anymore. Any rumors you may hear about me being sued for "brand destruction and defamation" are totally false. I can't control what anyone says about me; I can only control my response. And my response is to not respond at all, which, from what I can see so far, is the best way to deal with attention-seeking trolls who try to lift themselves up by putting others down.

Being half of a brand took all the joy out of performing. Now I'm writing my own songs for the first time, and I've fallen back in love with making music! I'm so lucky to have a new collaborator. She's an old and dear friend who has zero interest in global multi-platform domination. We're not in it for fame, fortune, or followers. Just fun. We've played a few of our songs for our biggest fans—shout-out again to Paisley and Maddy and also Kaytee and Alex and Harumi and Sofie-with-an-f—but I don't think we'll ever post them. I don't need that kind of attention anymore, and she never did. So please don't be disappointed if this is the last video I ever make.

My sister—who knows everything—says this won't be the last you'll see of me though. She predicts I'll show up in your feed doing something totally unexpected. Like winning an Olympic gold medal in fencing.

Morgan & Ella is over.

This is me—Ella Jane Plaza—*starting* over.

ABOUT THE AUTHOR

Megan McCafferty is the bestselling author of eleven novels for teens and tweens, including the Jessica Darling's IT List series. All her work is set in New Jersey, where she lives with her husband, son, and unofficial writing partner: a rescue dog named Louie who was cuddled beside her as she wrote this book. Like Ella, she loves to sing and prefers real life to social media, but you can find her online at meganmccafferty.com and @meganmccafferty on Twitter.